Beneath Burning Mountain

THERESA TOMLINSON

RED FOX

A Red Fox Book

Published by Random House Children's Books
20 Vauxhall Bridge Road, London, SW1V 2SA

A division of The Random House Group Ltd
London Melbourne Sydney Auckland
Johannesburg and agencies throughout the world

Copyright © text Theresa Tomlinson 2001

1 3 5 7 9 10 8 6 4 2

First Published by Red Fox 2001

The right of Theresa Tomlinson to be identified as the author of this work has been
asserted by her in accordance with the Copyright, Designs and Patents Act, 1988.

Printed and bound in Great Britain by
Bookmarque Ltd, Croydon, Surrey

Papers used by Random House are natural, recyclable products made from wood
grown in sustainable forests. The manufacturing processes conform to the environ-
mental regulations of the country of origin.

The Random House Group Limited Reg. No. 954009
www.randomhouse.co.uk

ISBN 0 09 940 9127

Contents

For Tom

1
Fish-faces

The fifth of July was a hot afternoon. I crouched down beside the bushes of plump bilberries, picking steadily while my fingers grew sticky. I stopped every now and then to lick up the sweet juice, but still my apron gathered new stains of deep red and purple. The waves lapped gently far below us, making me sleepy, while my brother and sister lolled in the springy heather, just creeping into flower.

"Get picking . . . yer lazy beggars!" I grumbled. "This is my birthday and it's supposed to be my day off, not yours!"

They both ignored me – they always ignored me. Joseph, who's the oldest, lay there scratching his fleabites while he chewed a tough stem of grass. I didn't really mind him so much, for I knew how he hated his stinking job, going round with the mule, picking up jugs of urine from folks' doorsteps and fetching it back to the alum works in barrels on the beast's back. A day away from that was bliss for him. Polly and me were grateful for a day away from helping Mam with her spinning, scouring and cooking. We were usually sent seaweed gathering in the afternoon.

Polly, who's our youngest, simply gazed out over the sea, gently wafting flies away from her face. "One of these days," she muttered, looking far down on to the little dock cut into the rocky shore, beneath the alum works, "one of these days I'm going to sail away from here and never come back again."

I stopped picking and sighed, rubbing my back and looking northwards towards the fine house that stood on the cliff

The Cranberry Girl

edge. "I'd never want to sail away from Burning Mountain," I told them. "But I'd like to live at Whingate Hall instead of Alum Row, and I'd like to wear fine clothes, instead o' patches."

They both exploded with laughter.

"Lady Nan!" Polly teased.

"Some chance of that!" said Joseph.

I returned to my picking. It wasn't fair – they always left the hard work to me. "I'm telling Mam," I complained. "You've done nowt to help . . . neither of you."

"Stop bleating Nanny Goat!" said Polly.

I gave up then and ignored them. My name is Anne and I don't mind being called Nan, but I hate it when they call me Nanny Goat. My shoulders ached from the picking, but I'd nearly filled our second best pudding basin. It would be all right, I told myself. Mam had promised me a honeyed bilberry pudding for my birthday supper, and she would know who'd done all the work; she only had to glance at the bright stains on my hands and clothes.

"Come on," I told them at last. "We're going back, there's still Mam's tea leaves to fetch."

"Come on then, Lady Nan," Joseph got up from the heather. "Take my arm and I'll lead thee down to Whingate Hall."

I didn't take his arm, I slapped him hard instead, but all he did was laugh.

Sir Rupert the Alum Master lived at Whingate Hall. He owned Burning Mountain where we worked and lived, as he owned all the land and sheep around us. But even though he was so very rich, he did not own the secret of alum making, and needed folk like my father and his brother Robert who'd been brought up knowing the mysteries of the work.

Whingate Hall was a beautiful stone built house with a fine

3

south-facing walled garden. We strode through the heather towards it, but as we drew near we had to take the side path that led round to the kitchen door. None of the alum workers would ever dare to go knocking on the front door, but we were regular visitors to the back. Dame Bunting, the sharp-witted cook, did a nice bit of business selling used tea leaves. They were dried on the stove and sold on to us for a few pence.

As we walked around the side of the house we heard lovely music and turned to look at the ballroom windows. The place blazed with lights, even though it was only mid-afternoon, and we could see young ladies in bright new gowns, dancing with fashionably dressed young men. I couldn't help but stand and stare; it looked so beautiful in there.

"Get on Lady Nanny Goat," said Polly grabbing my arm. "No dancing for thee."

"Mam says have yer got a twist o' tea leaves?" I asked politely when Dame Bunting opened the back kitchen door to us.

"I have that Miss Purple-Fingers," she said. "Just bide there while I fetch them, and don't touch anything. I'd have thought you'd all be working so early in t'afternoon."

"It's Nanny Goat's birthday," Polly told her mercilessly. "So Mam's given us the afternoon off."

"Bless thee lass," said Dame Bunting pressing a small packet of tea into my hand. "There's another fine birthday party going on *here* – Sir Rupert's youngest daughter, she's thirteen today."

"Exactly the same as me," I cried.

We left Whingate and set off home to Burning Mountain; I'd tea leaves in one hand and the bowl of berries in the other, but I couldn't help glancing back at the ballroom windows with longing. Then, as I turned round at last, something sharp shot through the air and caught me a stinging blow on the cheek. I gasped with shock and staggered, catching sight of an arm lashing fast as a whip, shaking the bushes down below us on the sloping cliff-side.

"Stones! Duck down!" Joseph shouted.

We ducked. Hoots of laughter came from the bushes, then a second stone grazed my hand. Mam's pudding bowl slipped from my grasp and crashed down at my feet. Joseph and Polly rose up from the grass, furious now.

"Damned Fish-faces!" Polly snarled. "I bet it's them."

I still clutched the tea leaves, though my wounded hand throbbed and a wave of sickness lurched up through my belly. Mam's bowl had broken into three pieces, spilling the precious berries everywhere.

"Stinking Fish-faces!" Joseph yelled as three big lads from Sandwick Bay shot up from the bushes, laughing fit to bust.

It was just too much; I couldn't keep back tears. Joseph shouted and waved his fist, but it was Polly who snatched up stones from the ground and marched fearlessly towards them. They smirked when they saw her coming, but as she went determinedly on, they began to back off. She pelted them, then bent to snatch up more.

"I'll show tha . . . I'll show tha," she bellowed. "We know yer Tommy Welford and we know yer mam."

The lads turned and walked away whistling as though they were simply out for a pleasant stroll. But they kept on going, moving away from us, skidding a little as they went back down the steep cliff-side towards Sandwick Bay, their tiny fishing village that clung to the cliffs north-west of the alum works.

Our Polly still followed them, screaming abuse at the top of her voice till Tommy Welford turned and stood his ground for a moment. "Raggy Piss-pourers!" he shouted, then he made a rude sign and ran to catch up with his mates.

"Tha's no right calling us names," Polly howled. "Yer mam

leaves a jug of piss out on your doorstep each morning. You want yer penny don't yer? Piss-sellers you are!"

She came back to us, red faced and angry. We three stood looking down at the broken bowl and spilled berries, mashed into the rocky ground.

"Best pick it up," said Joseph. "Mam might be able to fix it with a bit o' fishbone glue."

I bent to gather the pieces, swallowing hard. I scraped together some of the berries but it was hopeless, the soft fruit was squashed and caked with dirt. All my hard work for nothing.

"Well," Polly spoke with disgust, folding her arms. "No birthday supper for thee Nanny Goat."

We marched eastwards through sprawls of golden-flowered, sweet-smelling gorse that we call whins, then set off down hill, skirting the quarry that's cut from the cliff-side in the shape of a crescent moon. At mid-afternoon it was full of pick-men busy cutting and shovelling up the grey alum shale. We walked past three burning clamps that stood like giant charcoal stacks, forty feet high on a bit of level ground close by, so that the workers didn't have too far to go with their barrows. The barrow-men ran back and forth, feeding the smallest smoking clamp with oily fresh-mined alum shale, that turned dark red as it began to burn. The great piles burned away for three months at a time while clouds of sulphurous smoke rose from the top of the heaps, giving the place its name – Burning Mountain. We all believed that it was the foulness in that smoke that constantly turned our clothes to rags, so that our mothers sat by the fireside patching every night and we were known for our rag-tag clothes.

2

Run Like the Wind

Heavy with disappointment we continued our way down, treading carefully around the edge of the shallow steeping-pits where burnt shale lay soaking, turning the water red; it wouldn't do to go slithering into that. We went on, skidding down the cliff-side again, alongside the wooden channel that carried the steeped alum liquor downhill to the works. We passed more flowering whins and the manager's house standing at the head of Alum Row.

As the smell of stale urine grew, Polly pulled a face and wrinkled her nose. "No wonder they call us foul names," she complained.

"The less yer fuss, the less it bothers yer," I told her. "Well that's what Father says, anyway."

"Not true!" she replied. "Not when you've been away up there, breathing decent air for a while."

The smell was strongest by the warehouse, where large barrels of urine were kept; the staler it was, the better it worked. The stinking stuff would be poured into the boiled alum liquor and then boiled again to make the precious crystals form. Those crystals would fix dyes and soften leather so that woollen mills and tanneries paid good prices for them. Mam often complained that the money rarely reached the workers, but despite the terrible smells she insisted that it was a healthy place to live. "Perched up here like eagles on the cliffs," she'd say. Though we hated the sulphurous smoke that rose from the clamps and drifted down on to our cottages,

Alum Works

fisher-wives from Sandwick Bay would bring their coughing children up to breathe the fumes. "That smoke kills everything," Mam said. "It even kills whooping cough!"

Thomas Langtoft, our father, had the important job of watching the boiling pans and judging when the urine should be added. Father's skills were greatly respected even by the manager. His brother, Uncle Robert, had been invited to do the same job at Peak so that he and Aunt Margaret, who had no children and fussed us as though we were their own, had had to go over to Ravenscar to live. We missed them very much.

Our cottage on Alum Row was small, built on a wide cliff ledge above the ship dock and the cold North Sea. Us lasses longed for a cosy cottage like the ones by Sandsend Beck, all sheltered by Mulgrave Woods.

I stopped for a moment, looking back towards the smoking clamps above us. "What a place to live!" I sighed. "No wonder they call it Burning Mountain! No wonder they say that we're cursed!"

I'd feared Mam's anger when she saw the smashed bowl, but I needn't have worried about that. As we neared Alum Row we saw that something was wrong – something much worse than broken pots. There were no cries or shouting, but the coopers, the housemen, and the liquormen all started to run out of the work sheds and scramble up the steep cliff-side. The hens squawked and goats scattered in all directions as workers rushed through them like the wind.

Joseph grabbed both us lasses by the arm. "What is it?" he whispered.

The three of us watched open-mouthed as women hurried from their cottages in quiet panic, waving their arms and signalling to each other. I saw Father tear out of the boiler house and kiss Mam; then he climbed a little way up the steep bank. As we watched, he dived into one of the brick-built culverts which protect the channel that carries the alum liquor. Even Mr Douthwaite the manager ran out of the counting house and followed Father into the dark tunnel-like culvert.

Still nobody shouted or called and the strange quietness made me feel even more scared than if they'd been screaming at each other. Mam turned and saw us. She beckoned wildly and we started running down the path to meet her.

"What is it Mam?" Polly gasped, her voice shaking.

Mam hushed us, putting her finger to her lips, then took my arm. "Come and see," she whispered. She pulled me along with her, the other two following fast, heading for the ledge that overlooked the sloping cliffs to the east. We looked where she pointed and saw a great gang of burly men swarming over the rocks towards our small ship dock, pistols and cudgels in their hands.

Joseph pulled me sharply back from the edge. "The press-gang!" he hissed.

"Aye," Mam whispered. "Lyddy Welford told me they'd set themselves up in Grape Lane in Whitby. They've taken over that public house we call 'The Grapes' and they call it their rendezvous. Lyddy says there's a big ship and tender on the sea roads, hovering there out of sight, ready to take the men they capture down to the Thames."

A sudden rush of sickness lurched again, deep inside my stomach. The press-gang were more feared up on our cold stretch of coastline than constables or even pirates. Last time they'd come our way they'd carried Bess Tippet's dad off and her older brother too, taking them away to man the king's ships. Bess's family had never seen their menfolk again since the day the press-gang came. They'd had a terrible struggle to survive without them.

"What can we do?" I cried, really frightened now. I couldn't bear to have my father taken.

Mam shook her head, looking lost and scared herself. We followed her back towards the cottages and just as we got there our old neighbour Annie Knaggs stumbled out from her doorway dragging a heavy spade.

"Eeeh Annie – what're y' doing wi' that?" Mam asked.

Annie hauled the spade up on to her shoulder. "I'll give 'em a good thumping with it," she said. "I'll thump 'em hard if they come near any o' my lads!"

I didn't know whether to laugh or cry but Annie seemed to make Mam's mind up. "Ey Annie – tha's got the right idea!" she said, suddenly brave again. She rushed into our shack and snatched up her broomstick. "Nay!" she cried, "not that," flinging it on to the floor. Then she went to lift down from its nail, the sharp hand-scythe that Father used for cutting brushwood. "That's better!"

"What're yer going to do?" Joseph asked.

"Whatever we can," Mam was steely-eyed now. Then suddenly she looked thoughtful. "But I doubt it's our men they're really after," she said. "Our men know little o' seafaring ways!"

"Sandwick!" Joseph understood what she meant. "They're after the Sandwick men."

Polly was still angry with our attackers. "Smelly Fish-faces!" she cried.

We all knew that since the fighting with France had started up again, the press-gang were not too fussy who they took, but fishermen were a real prize for them; that way they'd get men already skilled with boats and weather and sailing winds. The press-gang would make a lot of effort to get a fisherman.

Polly folded her arms. "Tommy Welford and his mates have stoned our Nan and smashed our bowl. Let the press-gang taken 'em smelly Fish-faces – take the lot!"

Mam looked puzzled for a moment. Then she saw the shards of pot that I still clasped in my hands. "They stoned y' Nan?"

11

I nodded miserably. "Aye. That big lad, Tommy, Lyddy's boy."

Mam was not deterred. 'I'll speak to his mam about that I promise I will, but would you want his father carted off, taken away and never seen again? Would you want that?"

I hesitated, my cheek and hand still stinging.

"Nay," said Joseph firmly. "I'd not want that."

"Then run like the wind and warn 'em," said Mam. "Go to Lyddy – tell her we'll hold the gang up as best we can – and you must keep out of sight, our Joseph!"

"What!" I cried. "They'd not take Joseph! Haven't they got t' be eighteen?"

"They've taken lads before," Mam insisted. "They just have to look eighteen . . ." She shrugged her shoulders. "Now get on your way, all three of yer. One go to Top Green, one to Bottom Green, one to the staithe. Tell anyone – everyone! The first person you see."

We stared for a moment, miserable at the thought that we must run back almost the way we'd come and further still, but then Joseph snatched my hand and we were off, scrambling along the bankside towards Sandwick Bay.

Polly stumbled after us, still resentful. "And they called us Piss-pourers!" she growled.

We knew the winding pathway well, but I don't think we'd ever covered the ground so fast. I caught my foot in a rut, but pulled it out and staggered on while sharp stinging gorse prickles slashed my legs. Though I still smarted from the stoning that afternoon, a sense of urgency grew with every step. They didn't deserve us helping them like this – well, Tommy Welford didn't, but Joseph was right I'd hate to see his father carried off. There'd been many times when the Alum Master had not paid his workers properly and only a good parcel of Sandwick Bay herrings had saved us from hunger.

"Look!" Polly shouted, pointing back to Burning Mountain.

Joseph and I stopped and looked behind. The gang of men had reached our small dock and turned away from the sea, scrambling up towards Alum Row.

"They *are* looking for our men," I whispered.

"Aye," said Joseph smiling. "But see what greets 'em."

Then I saw what he meant. The rocky ledge that juts out beneath our homes was covered with women waving what looked like weapons but we knew must be spades, scythes, hoes and rakes.

As we watched the numbers grew.

Joseph laughed. "They're not going to get past that lot easy!"

"No," I agreed. "But come on! We've got no time t' waste!"

Joseph ran ahead but then suddenly skidded to a halt, pointing wildly out to sea. I couldn't understand what was wrong for a moment; then I saw what it was that bothered him. As the light began to fade and the sun sank down over the cliffs, there appeared on the seaward horizon a line of small black dots.

I grabbed Polly's arm and pointed. "The fishing boats," I cried.

As we stared at them the dots grew bigger, heading fast towards the staithe at Sandwick Bay.

"Coming back with the tide!" Polly said. "They won't know! We're too late!"

"No," Joseph cried, breaking into a run again. "We've got to get there."

"Run faster," I gasped at Polly. "Mam said run like the wind."

3

The First Person You See

We did run fast, faster than I had ever thought possible. My ankle ached and my throat hurt, but we were determined to get there and we did. Joseph went scrambling up the bank to Top Green, while Polly headed for the staithe. I hobbled up the dirt track that led to Bottom Green.

The first person you see? Mam's words echoed through my head, but all I could see were sleeping cats and a braying tied-up donkey. Then a door opened and Tommy Welford came out dragging an old fishing net behind him. He didn't even notice me, but sat down on his doorstep spreading the net out beside him, looking for holes.

"Oh no . . . it would be him!" I whispered. I drew breath and screamed at him. "Where's your mam?"

He leapt to his feet, mouth wide open, shocked at seeing me there, of all people.

"I never meant no harm," he cried. "It were nowt but larking, lass – just a lark!"

"Nay!" I gasped, finding it hard to get my breath and speak clear. "Not that! Not that! It's the press-gang. Press-gang coming – tell your mam."

He stared horrified for just one unbelieving moment, then he vanished inside the cottage, yelling for his mam.

I sat down on the Welfords' doorstep, gasping and rubbing my ankle. My side hurt too now, all of me hurt. But I heard the small tinny sound of a pan being beaten with a spoon, up at the top of the steep hill. Then Lyddy Welford threw open

14

her upstairs window above me, leaning out, banging her kettle with an iron ladle. "Press-gang! Press-gang!" she screamed.

Quickly she was answered by more clanging, followed by the thudding beat of a drum. The noise grew, windows and doors flew open, until at last a deafening row came from all around.

Tommy dashed past me banging wildly on an iron skillet, carrying the alarm down to the seafront and the little landing staithe. I picked myself up and followed him. The women flooded out of their houses, hammering for all they were worth on kettles, buckets, pans and drums, screaming and howling at the tops of their voices. "Press-gang! Press-gang! Turn about – turn about!"

The noise they raised was deafening, but we all stared anxiously out to sea. We made a huge row but we didn't know if it would be loud enough to carry warning over the grey rolling waves? The noise subsided while everyone watched, the low sun warm on our backs.

"They're still coming," said Tommy, a small uncertain catch in his voice.

"Try again!" his mother insisted, and once more the terrible din was raised. It came from the attics, the hilltop, the staithe below, and the banging of drums thundered across the sea. Then suddenly the boats seemed to have slowed their shoreward progress and were coming about.

A great cheer rang out, as we saw the boats turning against the tide. The boat-skills of the fishermen were great, no wonder the press-gang wanted them so much. Our warning had clearly been heard and understood.

"Right," Lyddy cried. "Now – lads, get thissens up into the woods!"

Everyone headed back up the hill. The boys who'd been too young to be out on the sea with their dads were sent up the bankside, towards the ravine and the thick green shelter of the woods. Baskets with bread and a bit of smoked fish were pushed into their hands, warm jerkins shoved beneath their arms. They'd have to stay out all night to be safe.

When at last the sounds of running feet had died away, Lyddy Welford came and hugged me tight. "Bless y' honey, for yer warning," she cried. Her cheeks were pink, her eyes full of tears.

Then she held me gently away, looking carefully at my face. "Tha's fair done in. Come inside and sit thissen down, I can see tha's limping! I've a pan o' good fish head stew still bubbling on my fire. Take a sup with me and rest that foot; the press-gang be damned!"

I was glad enough to do as she said, so I hobbled after her and sat down by her fire. I was soon given a bowl of steaming stew and I'd just raised the spoon to my mouth when Polly came knocking on the Welfords' door.

"You're here," she snapped. "I can't find Joseph anywhere."

"Well," said Lyddy, "if he's any sense he'll keep well away all through t' night, then creep back over the cliff tops. Here lass, settle down and have a sup, like yer sister."

Polly didn't need telling twice. I whispered to her under my breath, "I see tha's not so high and mighty that yer refuse the Fish-face's food."

Polly shrugged her shoulders and smacked her lips. "Shut tha mouth Nanny Goat! I'm starving and it smells so good!"

Again we settled to eat, but the cottage door banged open wide and Tommy followed by Joseph, rushed inside.

Lyddy flew up from her seat. "Still here? Why the devil aren't yer up there in t' woods?" she demanded.

"Too late!" Tommy cried. "They're here, swarming all over the village. We'll have to use our hole!"

"Aye! It's the only thing," his mother agreed, calmer now.

16

She slammed her own bowl down on the table and flung open the cupboard doors beneath the dresser. Tommy began hauling our roughly strewn fishing nets and old battered baskets, dumping them down on the cottage floor. The dresser was made of solid oak and built into the wall. Tommy reached in at the back and pulled out a light wooden panel that he handed to his mam.

"Tha's seen nowt o' this!" she spoke fiercely to us.

"No nowt," we hurried to reassure her. We were awed and silent, knowing that we were being trusted with a big secret. Though everyone knew that most of the fishing families did a bit of smuggling on the side, as did the alum workers, we'd never seen proof before. We never asked about secret hiding places, so the knowledge of how it was done was kept very quiet.

Tommy dived into the bottom of the cupboard and vanished from view.

"Yer must get in too, Joseph," Lyddy Welford insisted. "Yer mam'd not forgive me if they took you instead o' our lad!"

Joseph hesitated, but the sounds of banging and shouting out in the narrow yard made him duck his head and scramble quickly into the small dark space after Tommy.

Lyddy Welford pushed the loose panel firmly back into place so that it looked just like the solid back of the cupboard, then we all stooped down with shaking hands to pile the old fishing nets and baskets back in.

A loud crash close by told us that the press-gang had reached the cottage next door.

"What can we do?" I whimpered.

"Sit down and eat as though nowt be wrong!" Lyddy Welford told us.

4
Nowt but Lasses!

So though we shook with fear, we did as she said. No sooner had we raised our spoons once more than the cottage door was thrust open and two big men swinging cudgels burst in. One of them grabbed me by the shoulders, staring closely at my face. He stank of ale and tobacco and roughly shoved my bonnet back.

"Wench!" he snarled, disappointed.

The other snatched hold of Polly and pulled up her skirt,

Polly's clog came up sharply and kicked his shin. "I mightn't be a lad, but I'll fight like one," she growled.

"Damned bitch!" the man groaned, lifting his hand to slap her.

"I'd not do that if I were thee!" Lyddy Welford cried, taking up the kettle of boiling water from her fire. "There's nowt but lasses here, so be on yer way!" She was a big angry woman, with powerful arm muscles and she looked as though she'd use that kettle if she had to. I knew that most of the village lads had felt her hand on their ear at one time or another.

The men hesitated for a moment, glaring peevishly around the room. They pushed the settle aside and pulled open the cupboard doors. One of them dragged out an old basket and flung it on the floor. "Rubbish!" he muttered.

"Nowt in *this* place is rubbish," Lyddy growled.

The bigger man looked as though he'd a mind to tip the settle right over, but he glanced back at Lyddy again and seemed to change his mind.

"Come on," said one. "There's nowt for us here. I want m' dinner. They'll have brought the carts to t' bank-top by now. I'm off back t' rendezvous."

The other fellow was not so willing to leave, he moved towards the table still rubbing his shin where Polly had kicked him. "There's some dinner here for thee," he grinned nastily.

Lyddy put down the kettle and snatched up one of the bowls of stew instead. "Yer can have it on yer head!" she promised. "Tha'll not have it in tha belly!"

"Bitches!" the big man spat out, but he backed away towards the door. He could see that nothing would be gained easily. He lashed out with his cudgel and knocked a flower-painted pot from the dresser, so that it smashed on to the floor. Then suddenly they'd gone, and all was quiet. Polly and I sank down on to the wooden settle, hugging each other tightly with relief.

"Damn them, that was my best bit o' china," said Lyddy. "Never mind . . . it's nowt to the thought o' losing my Francis or Tommy. That's my brave lasses," she praised us warmly. "Tha's both done very well with that."

"Can't stop shaking," I gulped.

"A good meal is what's needed, though we've been at a deal o' trouble to get it. Sit down again and I'll ladle out some fresh hot stew."

She brought steaming bowls to us and scraped the cold food back into her pot. This time we did manage to eat our fill, and the rich fishy gravy warmed and cheered us.

"Mam, Mam," Tommy called from the cupboard, his voice faint. "Let us out now? We're cramped an' hungry."

Lyddy winked at us. "Just a moment or two, my lads. Just a moment more to make sure those damned fellows've gone right away."

As soon as it was really dark, with the oil lamp lit and

shutters closed, Lyddy let the lads out of their hidey-hole and gave them their supper. They came out grumbling and groaning at their cramped muscles and empty bellies.

"Yer must all stay here till morning," Lyddy said. "And don't step outside this door; I don't trust those fellows, not one bit."

"This bread is dry and the stew's cold," Tommy complained.

"Better than what your father'll get!" his mother told him sharply.

Tommy hung his head then, understanding that his father and the other fishermen would be out at sea all night, with nothing to eat or drink or warm them. "Aye," he nodded.

"Must they stay out all night?" I asked.

Lyddy nodded. "If they want to be safe they will, and they'll be desperate tired and cold by morning, wi' their catch o' fish starting to waste. Still, better than being carried off by that lot. Now then, you two lasses'd best come and sleep in my big bed wi' me. Joseph, I'll set a mattress down here, so yer can sleep wi' Tommy beside the fire."

I was expecting Polly to fuss, but she didn't. We stripped down to our petticoats and fell into the Welfords' lumpy bed with relief.

"What a day," I whispered. "M' birthday too!" It seemed ages since we were picking bilberries, though my fingers still carried purple stains. I gently touched my cheek where it still smarted from the stone.

"Get to sleep," murmured Polly. We both slept as through we'd never wake again.

Lyddy had us all up and the shutters open as soon as the first rays of light showed in the east. She made us porridge and while we were eating it she crept out into the quiet streets.

Tommy kept looking at me while I ate, making me feel a bit fussed.

"What's up with thee?" Polly snapped. "Stop staring at our

Nan like that!"

Tommy put out his hand and I saw that it shook. He touched my sore cheek awkwardly, but very gently. "Did I do that?"

"You did," I nodded.

"And yer called us bad names," Polly insisted.

He went red in the face and looked down at his bowl for a moment, but then spoke up firmly. "I'm sorry," he said. "It were . . . ignorant, ignorant o' me."

I looked at him doubtfully, wondering if this was another of his larks, but he turned away still blushing and I saw that perhaps he did really mean it.

"I promise yer this, Nan Langtoft," he said, his voice low. "I'll never do ought like it again."

"Not to anyone?" I asked quietly.

He looked surprised for a moment. Then he answered me. "Not to anyone."

All four of us ate on in silence, then suddenly Tommy lent across and kissed my sore cheek. Both Joseph and Polly exploded with laughter. I must have blushed beetroot red then, for I know I went all hot and couldn't think what to do or say.

Just then Lyddy came back in through the door. "Well, I'm glad you bairns can still laugh after the night we've had. It all seems quiet out there, and I see the boats coming back."

"Will they be safe now?" I asked.

"Aye. We must pray so, lass, and we must see that thee and tha brother and sister get home safely to Burning Mountain. Tommy! Walk over the sands wi' them, and make sure that all is well."

"Aye," Tommy gave a quick nod.

5

Behind Starhole Rocks

We set off from Sandwick Bay, walking eastwards along the sands, sparkling waves lapping beside us, the sun warm on our faces. It was a beautiful fresh morning and we could see the fishing boats coming back. The two lads walked in front of us lasses, talking and kicking pebbles, they seemed to be thinking much more kindly of one another since they'd had their frightening wait together, cooped up in the back of the Welfords' cupboard.

Polly kept digging me in the ribs with her elbow. "He's sweet on thee," she whispered, nodding at Tommy.

"Hush tha mouth!" I told her. "He wasn't sweet on me yesterday morning."

The sand was smooth and fresh where the tide had washed it, but as we wandered on I suddenly saw something that turned me ice cold. A patch of sand ahead of us, close to Starhole Rocks, was patterned with deep footprints. I stopped, trembling as I stood there. I couldn't take another step.

"What is it?" Polly asked.

I nodded my head in the direction of the rocks. "Footprints," I hissed. "Masses of them, coming down from the bankside."

Polly looked and saw what I meant. Then even worse, I noticed a pair of large booted feet, sticking out from behind Starhole Rocks. Somebody was hiding there and beside them on the sand lay a stack of cudgels and a pair of pistols.

"Joseph!" I called, my voice low and shaking.

He turned and must have seen the fear in my face. "Summat up!" he told Tommy. They both came back to us fast.

"The gang," I whispered. "Behind Starhole Rocks."

Both lads looked for themselves, and saw what I had seen. Then while we stood in stunned silence, we heard the murmur of voices and a low laugh.

"Waiting for the fleet!" Tommy gulped. "I must go back! You go on home! They'll not follow yer if they think they can get our men!"

He turned at once and ran back to Sandwick Bay. We three stared at each other for a moment, unsure what to do, then we set off after him, tearing along the beach once more, towards the returning boats. Suddenly all pretence of hiding was done. The press-gang realised what we were up to and came after us, like dogs after a rabbit, cursing and swearing for all they were worth.

Tommy reached the staithe ahead of us and stood there waving his arms frantically, "Turn about! Turn about!"

We joined him pointing and screaming so that they looked and saw the press-gang streaming after us. The boats were so near that we could see the weariness in the men's faces, but they quickly understood our frantic signals and turned about. One of the fishermen struggled to the stern and looked as though he'd jump out and wade towards us, but his friends dragged him back. I knew then that the man was Francis Welford, Tommy's dad, and my heart sank as I heard the howls of rage behind us. The press-gang, furious that we'd given warning, had snatched Tommy and our Joseph instead of the men that they were really after.

"Damned brats!" they bellowed. "We'll take thee instead of thy fathers!"

I screamed, "Yer cannot take them, they're nobbut lads."

"Big lads these! They looked eighteen to us! They'll do for now!" the angry men growled.

"Give him back! Give him back!" Polly shrieked and grabbed Joseph's arm. "He's only fourteen."

One of the men swung round and slapped her face hard, grinning with satisfaction. He was the man that she'd kicked yesterday, and it was clear that he'd been longing to do that ever since. "Oh he'll enjoy his life as a cabin boy, missy! Tha'll not know him when he comes back to thee! If ever, that is!"

Polly fell with a thud amongst the shingle and I crouched down at her side, trying to protect her from the trampling feet. When I glanced up again I saw that the men were forcing open Tommy's tight closed fist. He resisted for all he was worth, but they were so much stronger than him and at last they pressed a dirty shilling coin into his palm.

"Done!" they cried. "Taken the king's shilling! That's one impressed. Now the other."

Joseph was given the same treatment and the two boys were hauled off up the bank, jolted and shoved at every step. The commotion brought the old men and fishwives, shocked and bewildered, out from their cottages. When they saw what was happening they began to protest fiercely, but the press-gang were determined that they should take somebody back with them. Anyone who interfered received a swift swing of a cudgel. The boys were dragged off up the hill, followed by angry women hurling abuse at them. Though I wanted to go too, I knew that I must see Polly safe.

She lay there on the pebbles, white-faced, her mouth bleeding and swelling fast, so I went to the fresh water where the beck trickled into the sea and dipped my stained apron into the cleanest part. When I returned to her, Polly was struggling to get up.

"Oh, Nan," she whispered. "Have they got our brother?"

"Aye," I murmured. "They have."

24

The Sandwick women found us huddled together on the staithe, when they came back down the hill. Their voices were hushed and gentle now, though their faces were white, shocked at what had happened. Lyddy Welford took us both by the hand and insisted that we go back to her cottage. She made us sit down and have a sip of warm ale with herbs in it. Other women followed after us, crowding into her small home-place.

"Wh . . what should we do?" I asked.

For once Lyddy had no answer. She shook her head and stroked Polly's hair. I saw that the knuckles on her big strong hand were bruised and the skin torn. One of the press-gang had certainly felt her fist and I was glad at least of that.

We sat there for a while still stunned, the women full of sighs and angry muttering, then at last Lyddy got up. "I shall take these lasses back to Burning Mountain," she said. "Their mother must be told what's happened, and their father too." She sighed. "I hate to do it, but I think I'd best do the telling."

The women agreed reluctantly and began to wander back to their own homes, arms folded, faces grim.

It was a sad slow walk back home. We spoke little and I still hobbled, while Polly's cut face began to swell. All seemed calm at Burning Mountain; a few seaweed gatherers were down on the beach, for Father was working hard to find a way of using kelp, instead of the hated urine, as we knew some other works did. Annie Knaggs was at her usual task burning the stuff in a small kiln, then she'd collect the ashes and carry them up to the works.

When we walked through our cottage door Mam stopped her spinning wheel and jumped up, rushing to hug us.

"What happened? Where've you been? I've been so fearful," she cried. Then she looked properly at Polly's face. "What's this?" she cried. "I feared summat like this!"

We just shook our heads for we could not speak.

6
Lady Hilda, Help Us!

When Lyddy followed us inside and stood awkwardly by the door Mam knew that there was something terribly wrong.

"Joseph?" she called, pushing past us to the doorway.

"Mary. I'm terrible sorry," Lyddy whispered, catching her arm.

"No," Mam whispered. "Not my Joseph. They've not taken my lad?"

Lyddy nodded.

Mam was aghast. "How could yer let them Lyddy? When I sent my own bairns to give warning?"

Lyddy just stood there sorrowful and silent.

"T'wain't Lyddy's fault," I whispered. "She did all she could t' look after us – and their Tommy's been taken along with our Joseph."

"What? Tommy too?"

"Aye," Lyddy whispered. "Tha's three brave children Mary," she went on. "Without their warning we'd ha' lost all our men. Because o' them none of our fellows is taken, they're all staying out in the sea roads."

Mam went to Lyddy then full of shared sorrow, flinging her arms around the fisherwoman. They clung together, tears pouring down both their faces. Polly and me crept outside, leaving them be.

The news of the two lads' capture spread fast around the Alum Works. Father stopped his work and came home with many of the workers following him. Henry Knaggs, our neighbour, left his barrow and came down from the spoil heaps to see what was up. They gathered about our cottage door, their voices low with concern. Mr Douthwaite came to ask why work had stopped, and when he was told, even he turned away with no complaints and went quietly back to the counting house.

"They'll be keeping them in the back room at The Grapes," said Henry. "My grandmother lives close by and she can hear the poor fellows complaining and banging on the bars they've had put int' windows."

"Aye," Bart Little, the smith, agreed. "They'll be there a day or two mebbe, then they row 'em out to the tender, and that's the last y' see of 'em . . . unless you're very lucky."

Father looked sharply at the men, beginning to see what they meant. "So there's a day or two before they carry them off to the Thames?"

"Maybe longer," Henry told him. "Depends how fast they can fill up their tender. I hear they're causing a deal o' havoc but I don't believe they're having much success. I'd swear that's why they took your lads, they're getting desperate."

We were all quiet at the thought of the two boys locked up like that, but we knew that even worse would await them on a man o' war. If the fighting didn't get them, the fever most likely would.

Suddenly father spoke up firmly. "I'll go to Whitby. It cannot be right that they take lads o' fourteen."

"Nay," Lyddy whispered, "they're nobbut bairns."

Henry shook his head. "All protections 're cancelled," he told them. "They're not worth the paper that they're written on. They're calling it an emergency, this threat from the fellow they call Napoleon Buonaparte, and even boatswains and harpooners can be taken off the whaling ships."

"Tha'll not be going Thomas," Mam told Father, pointing

a determined finger at him. "They'd clap you straight into their back room along wi' the lads. No, I shall go instead."

Father shook his head, looking thoughtful for a moment, then suddenly hopeful. "That's it," he cried. "I shall go and offer myself in return for the two lads."

"No you *will not*!" Mam bellowed, her upset turned to anger. "That way I'd be sure to lose thee both."

"Mary's right," said Lyddy. "You cannot do deals with those fellows Thomas. They'd snap yer up as well as the lads. No, Mary is right enough, and if she goes, I'll go with her. We can put up as good an argument as thee, and at least they'll not want us for their ships."

Though Father was unhappy about it Mam was determined. She got up early next morning and dressed herself with care. She put on her Sunday gown and bonnet, a spotless apron and her one pair of good boots that she'd polished till they shone. When we saw what she was about, Polly and I quietly started to dress ourselves in our Sunday clothes as well.

"What are you lasses up to?" Mam demanded, when she saw what we did.

"We're coming too," I told her.

"You'll not," she insisted. "Father, tell these lasses they're not to follow me."

"Nay Father," I insisted. "Tell Mam that we *must* go, for what if ought should happen to her, who'll come back here and fetch help?"

Father looked bewildered for a moment.

"This is no holiday jaunt," Mam told us.

"We know that," said Polly. "We're not bairns – neither Nan nor me."

Father heaved a great sigh. "There is something in what they say, Mary. Will you promise me this, my lasses, that you'll not set foot in that dreadful rendezvous place, but wait safely outside for your mother to come back out again?"

"Aye, we will," we both agreed.

"Then Mary," he said. "I think that they're right. It's true what they say. They didn't act like bairns yesterday, did they? They may be a good help to thee."

Mam sighed. "Aye well, remember what you've promised. I cannot bear to have another of my bairns taken from me. Tha'd best come quickly then, for I've promised to meet Lyddy at Bank Top in time for the carrier's cart."

Going to Whitby in the carrier's cart would be a treat on any other day. We set off rattling along the rough coast road, past packhorses laden with seaweed and wagons full of fish. I turned about and saw in the distance behind us, the tiny figures of the alum miners, running with heavy barrows from the quarry to the burning clamps, from the burning clamps to the steeping-pits. They looked like ants, running back and forth all over the cliff-face that was cut into terraces and round the bottom of the smoking clamps. I could see the piled-up shale turning red as it burnt, and the men opening up one of the great piles that had finished burning, so that we could see its deep red heart torn apart. On any other day I'd be thrilled to be getting away from the stink and hard work, to breathe the fresh clean air of the moors.

Polly sitting beside me looked pale and determined, and I felt a touch of shame that I should be thinking of anything other than our Joseph. What would it have been like for him, to spend the night locked up in that place? Then I thought of Tommy, and touched the place on my cheek. It was still sore, but I remembered the gentle kiss that had followed and knew that I didn't want Tommy taken away any more than our Joseph.

"All out!" the carrier cried, as we reached Lythe Bank.

Most of the passengers grumbled, but we got down obediently.

Polly stretched her back. "That's better," she smiled, but then she caught Mam's solemn face. "Are you scared Mam?" she asked.

Mam looked as though tears might well up again, she couldn't speak, just shook her head.

"Aye lass," Lyddy answered for them both. "We're scared. But we're more scared that we'll fail to bring our lads back, than of ought that those villains might do to us."

We set off walking down the hill, relieved to stretch our legs. All the carriers made their passengers get out and walk at that point, for many a laden cart had come to grief, so steep was the winding bank at Lythe. Once it was emptied, the man led the strong Cleveland Bays round to the back of the cart and fastened them up again. We could not help but slither a bit as we followed the carrier, walking beside his horses, using their weight as a brake. As we rounded the bend we caught our first glimpse of Whitby in the distance and the beautiful broad sweep of white sands that stretch from Sandsend to Whitby harbour.

"Not far now," Polly said pointing ahead. "I can see St Hilda's Abbey in the distance."

"Lady Hilda help us!" Mam whispered.

"Amen to that," Lyddy spoke with feeling and we all went quiet again.

Fishermen

7

Down Grape Lane

I always loved arriving in Whitby. We got out of the cart and walked along the harbour side, breathing in the strong smell of fish, enjoying the bustle and arguments over fish prices. I stared across the harbour up to the ancient abbey ruins that loomed above us now.

Beneath the Abbey Cliffs and church stood Henrietta Street, with its gaping spaces where once fine houses had stood. They'd been lost in the terrible landslip that had carried many dwellings down into the harbour a few years ago. Along the north-east coast we had regular slips of land; we all lived with the fear of it, and mostly they were small, but just now and again it would happen quite suddenly and a large lump of cliff would go crashing down into the sea.

Lyddy and Mam looked at each other, suddenly uncertain now that they'd got there.

"What shall we do?" said Lyddy. "Staring up at the abbey's no good. Shall we go straight to Grape Lane and demand they return our children or round to Frank's cousin Hester's? She'll give us a bite to eat and a sup o' ale?"

"My stomach's heaving so I couldn't eat or drink. Best get it done wi'," said Mam, her voice shaky. "I doubt the constable will interfere, I hear the gang have been taking whoever they want. Let's get it done."

So then we turned about and walked off fast, towards the bridge. The Grapes public house, that the press-gang called their rendezvous, had a reputation for dirt and rough behaviour. Men with cudgels and pistols stuck in their belts stood around outside, swigging back drink and smoking their pipes. Two open barrels were set up at the back of the bridge, and as we passed them the stench told us their purpose. This was the Whitby method of urine collection. People brought their chamber pots to empty into the barrels and they weren't always particular whether they spilled it or not.

Polly pinched her nose. "That stuff'll probably be sent to Uncle Robert at Peak Works," she said. "Though Father told me they're beginning to use a lot o' kelp there instead."

"See him," I nudged her and nodded her head towards the rendezvous. "He's the one who knocked yer down."

"Let me near him!" Polly growled.

"I certainly won't!"

He was lounging against the wall and laughing; I remembered his foul breath in my face. I slowed my steps, fighting the urge to run. I knew that this was no adventure.

Mam turned round, her voice sharp and threatening. "Right now, lasses y'd better do as yer promised yer father. Stand over there by Maggie Megginson's fish stall and don't move from her side. Yer can see all who go in and out from there."

My heart was thumping and a terrible urge to spew grew in my stomach. I was glad enough to go and stand beside the sturdy fishwife, out of the way. Mam and Lyddy gathered themselves together and marched quickly past the men's foul insults, up the steps and into the rendezvous.

I grabbed hold of Polly's hand. The fishwife turned to smile at us. "Now then lasses, Mary Langtoft's bairns from Burning Mountain, aren't tha?"

"Aye," we nodded.

"What brings thee into Whitby Town? Can I sell thee a fresh codling or summat?"

We shook our heads. "Mam has told us to bide here."

"If that's all right with you Maggie?" I added.

"Aye course it is," Maggie laughed. "Where is it Mary's gone?"

"She's gone with Lyddy Welford," I told her. "Into 'The Grapes'."

"Eeh now!" Maggie laughed. "Whatever are they doing in there?"

"They've gone to see about our Joseph and Tommy Welford. They've been taken by the press-gang and they're only fourteen."

Maggie's laughter fled. "Eh lasses," she whispered softly. "I'm right sorry to hear that." She frowned at the news and looked worried. "Here!" she said, "take these." She pushed warm boiled crab claws into our hands for us to suck.

I don't think we had to wait very long, but the time seemed to drag. We sucked politely at our crab claws but the more I sucked the sicker I felt. Maggie sold her fish steadily. Respectable Quaker dames came and went, dressed in plain gowns with black scarves about their shoulders. I stared at them, they were so clean and though they'd clearly got money they didn't send their servants out to do the shopping. Farmer's wives with baskets full of vegetables cried their wares all about us. Each woman that came to Maggie's stall was told why we were waiting there.

"Poor bairns!"

"They never have! Fourteen years old – nobbut lads?"

Shocked whispers flew around and we were treated to many sympathetic glances.

"They'll have all gone to get 'em out o' the rendezvous!" one woman muttered. "Once they're locked up in that back room," she shook her head. "They've set up iron bars at the windows!"

"It's not right," one customer declared. "They'll be taking bairns in clouts next."

Another woman who brought smoked herrings to the stall

for Maggie to sell glanced furiously across the street to where the men lounged. "They make our lives a misery," she hissed.

"Aye, they do that right enough!" Maggie agreed.

"Our Samuel's hiding away back in t' yard, getting under my feet and making me nattered. He no sooner came back from Greenland and stepped off his whaling boat than the gang arrived and set up over there. Now I daren't let the lad out on t' street for fear they take him. At the slightest hint of trouble I make him shin up our chimney, so I can't get much of a fire going either!"

I looked about me then and saw what she said was true. Whitby did seem rather quiet and those around were mainly women and old men. Where were all the boat-builders, fishermen, whalers that usually thronged the streets?

Maggie clicked her tongue in disapproval. "Tha wouldn't mind so much if they'd treat 'em fair and give decent pay, but they say it's a living death on them stinking ships. It's more likely the sickness gets 'em than the fighting. They'd not stand for ought like this in France."

The woman laughed. "In France it's not the king they serve, it's folk like thee and me. Maybe they treat their sailor lads better now that their king may whistle for his head."

"Oh I don't know as this Napoleon fellow's much different to a king," said Maggie more gently. "At least our king's not wild wi' his money. They say he wain't eat sugar, and forbids it at court; all to help the poor slaves and stop the slavers getting rich on sugar cane."

"Nay, don't believe it! He just wain't spend the money and he's going mad again! They've called those Willis doctors in again I hear!"

But Maggie wouldn't have it. "I'd rather have Farmer George for king than his son, I can tell y' that."

"Eeeh I'd gladly do away wi' both," the woman replied. "If I'd been there when they pulled that Bastille down, I'd have been first inside. It's a shame we've no Bastille I say."

The woman's face was very grim. A shiver ran down my back for I suddenly knew that she really meant what she said.

"Aye," said Maggie suddenly thoughtful. "True we've no Bastille, but we've got that place," she nodded her head towards the press-gang's rendezvous.

All at once their conversation was interrupted by the sound of raised voices and shouting. Mam and Lyddy appeared. They were escorted roughly down the steps of the rendezvous and thrust towards the muddy gutter that ran down the middle of the street.

"Bide here by me!" Maggie hissed and caught my hand in hers. Then she turned to the kipper woman who she'd been talking to. "If you clap eyes on Hester Welford, tell her that her cousin's wife's in a bit o' bother."

"I'll go directly to fetch her," the woman spoke low and at once set off down the street.

"My Mam!" Polly cried aloud in outrage, seeing our mother treated so disrespectfully.

Mam and Lyddy turned on their escort with clenched fists and loud complaints, but the press-gang's lieutenant strolled over towards them, leering. Suddenly pistols were drawn all about the two women and the lieutenant was growling at them in a low voice. We could not hear clearly, but there was mention of the constable and the stocks. I saw Lyddy take Mam by the arm and back away. The lieutenant roared with laughter, as did some of the other men, but many of the Whitby folk stopped their work and chatter, standing in grim silence watching. Even the traders paused in their selling, showing little mirth at the sight of two desperate mothers so roughly treated and insulted.

"'Tis their sons the gang have taken," Maggie whispered. "Two lads barely fourteen."

"Two lads!" low voices repeated it up and down the street.

8

Something's Going to Happen

At last Mam and Lyddy came over towards us dusting themselves down, red faced and angry. "Oh Mam!" Polly cried, grabbing her arm. "Have they hurt you? We've been so scared."

"We've failed our bairns," Mam's voice turned shaky, her hands trembling. "That's what natters me most. They say it's up to us to prove our lads under age, they'll not take our word for it."

Lyddy was shaking too. "They're threatening us all ways. If we make more fuss they'll fetch the constable and have us put in the stocks," she said. "They claim they've orders from t' Admiralty, all protections cancelled. How can we prove their ages, if they'll not take their own mothers' word for it?"

"I believe they'll take sworn statement from a parish priest," Maggie tried to help.

"Aye," Mam agreed. "But they'll have sent the lads off to the Thames before we can get that done."

"Eeeh Lyddy, whatever are you up to?" A small woman in a fishing bonnet came shoving her way through the crowds towards us.

"Hester?" Lyddy flung her arms about her husband's cousin, and all talking at once, we tried to explain what had happened.

Hester looked worried. "We mun get you out of here," she told us. "Come back home wi' me. This here press-gang are more vicious and feared than any other that's come our way.

All protections ignored they say, and they're even taking the lads off the whaling ships. Isn't that true Maggie?"

"Aye, right enough," Maggie agreed.

Mam's eyes flashed and her voice was firm and angry. "It cannot be right that they take such young lads."

"No, honey," Maggie agreed. "Whatever t' Admiralty says, I say it's wrong, and there's plenty round here would agree wi' me. But your Hester speaks true; there's nowt else thi can do now. Go and rest at her cottage, tha's both done in."

Lyddy nodded her head, distressed, but seeing the sense in it.

Maggie bent forwards and touched her shoulder. "This ain't the end Lyddy. There's many a whisper flying about these yards. Many a strong man cramped away in hidey-holes, desperate to burst out. Like a tinder box Whitby is, just wanting a match."

Mam and Lyddy listened thoughtfully, a touch of hope seeming to creep back into their eyes.

"I speak truth," Maggie nodded. "Whitby's like to flare up and burst into flames. All due to them!" She spat furiously and dipped her head towards the men of the press-gang, who'd gathered together and were climbing into a cart.

We all went quiet then, staring at Maggie, wondering just what her words might mean.

Hester broke in. "Come thy ways," she told us firmly, so we nodded and followed her obediently up Kirkgate and into Welfords' yard.

"Y' mun stay the night, there's room in our attic," Hester insisted.

Mam shook her head, wondering what to do. "I can't go back without Joseph, but Thomas will be worried sick. I'm feared he'll come looking for us and get himself impressed too."

"The carrier'll take a message," Hester told her. "Though he'll be setting off at noon and that can't be far away."

"We can find him," I offered. "Me an' Polly."

"Good lasses," Hester nodded. "It's a strange day I say, when lasses are safer on the streets than lads."

Mam looked a little uncertain, but Lyddy put an arm round each of us. "They'll be fine. Yer should've seen them yesterday," she said. "Ready to take on the press-gang single-handed they were."

Lyddy's praise made me feel stronger, so when Mam nodded, I grabbed Polly and we rushed outside before she changed her mind.

We went fast up Kirkgate towards the White Horse and Griffin, for we knew that the carrier would be stabling his horse there. It was one of the main setting-off spots for coaches and carrier's carts, travelling in and out of Whitby.

"We've not got long," I said, grabbing Polly and breaking into a run. The sun was high in the sky above us and we were just in time for the bell was ringing, warning passengers that the carrier was about to set off.

"Please tell Father that we're safe and staying here the night," I cried as the coach rumbled out of the yard.

"I will my lass, if I can get out of Whitby through this lot," the carter shouted back to us.

It was only then that we really saw what he meant. We'd been so frantic to find our man that although we'd been pushing past people we'd not really noticed how many there were out on the streets now. The crowds usually built up a bit in the afternoon, but this gathering was different. The market traders were quiet for once, with few customers looking at their wares. Instead many women, both young and old, seemed to be milling around the rendezvous and the opening of Grape Lane. We could see the carter ahead of us, battling his way across the bridge. When people noticed him they moved aside, willing enough to let him through.

The uncomfortable feeling that I'd had as I'd listened to Maggie talking to her friends earlier came creeping back to me. "Summat's going to happen," I whispered.

"Aye," Polly agreed, slipping her arm through mine and moving closer. "Is it summat bad?"

"Don't know."

I couldn't think why we both felt so scared, but then I realised that what was so strange was the quietness of the crowd. People were talking, but their voices were low, almost with church-like softness. A great deal of whispering and signing went on from window to doorway, from trader to shopkeeper and back again.

Then there was a stir in the crowd at the bridge-end, and an old man climbed on to a stool, close to Maggie's stall. He was shaky in the legs and had to be held up by Maggie but as he began to speak all heads turned towards him.

"It's William. Old William!" The whisper flew around. "What's he up to?"

We pushed slowly forwards, trying to catch what the old man said. Polly kept tight hold of my hand.

We couldn't hear him clearly but even the whispering stopped while people struggled to hear. The man waved his fist and pointed down Grape Lane to the rendezvous. We pushed closer so that we too could see down the lane, as all heads turned to glare at two armed guards, standing on the steps of the timbered building. They glanced at each other in sudden alarm, then fled inside, closing the doors tight shut behind them.

Polly and I wriggled forwards again, straining our ears to hear.

"Look about thi," William cried. "What do y' see? Where are yer men? They live in hiding."

There was much agreement, and cries of "Aye! Aye, they do!"

40

"Skilled whaling men's been taken, harpooners and even youngsters! This gang has turned Whitby into a place of fear. We'll treat this rendezvous as the French did their Bastille!"

"Aye! Aye! We will!" Angry muttering rose.

"Now's the moment!" We heard Maggie's voice raised. "Now, before they get back wi' their weapons and their victims. No more stolen Whitby lads I say!"

"No!" The quiet broke and roars of angry agreement came from all around. There was a sudden surge of movement down the lane as the furious crowd of old men and women rushed towards The Grapes Hotel, hurtling themselves at its door.

9

Our Own Bastille

As angry women streamed past us I was terrified and delighted both at once.

"Hooray!" Polly yelled, her face flushed, eager to join in now.

I hauled her back, fearful that she'd dash into the middle of the throng. "No," I told her. "We ought t' go and fetch Mam!"

"It'll all be over and we'll miss it," she cried. She was carried away by the wild determination about her now, and didn't seem to see the danger.

Great crashes and thuds reached us as the doors of the rendezvous were battered and thumped. The men left behind to guard the place broke the small glass panes and fired shots from the windows, so that the attackers were forced to turn and fight their way back up the lane. It went quieter then, and the women seemed to be struggling in all directions.

"Is it over?" I whispered.

Then shouts rang out behind us and all at once a second, more powerful wave of rebellion began. Suddenly the men were there, pouring out of the yards and alleyways. News of what was happening had flown through the town so that cooped-up seafarers joined their women folk, with anger in their hearts and homemade pikes in their hands. Strong men from whaling ships broke free from the misery of their cramped hidey-holes, pushing past us, joining the attack with gusto. I knew there'd be no stopping them. The doors were quickly broken open and the guards disarmed.

"T' prisoners – fetch 'em out!" the cry went up.

I didn't know whether to run for Mam or stay to see what happened.

"What about Joseph?" Polly wailed.

"Aye, we must find him," I agreed, still unsure what to do for the best. But then we saw that people nearby were pointing upwards to the rooftops, and as we watched we saw young men and lads pop out of one of the chimneys, high above The Grapes Hotel. A trail of sooty fugitives went clambering and skidding across the rooftops, leaping fast from neighbouring house to house, down towards the farthest end of the lane that would lead them back to Kirkgate.

"Joseph, that's him!" Polly cried.

"Aye, and there goes Tommy," I shouted, then all at once my eyes filled up with tears and I could not see clearly any more. I don't know whether they were tears of relief that they were out or fear for what might happen next.

"What shall we do?" Polly asked me.

I dashed the tears away and tried hard to think. "If we run back up Crossgate we'll maybe meet them back on Kirkgate."

We turned around and hurried back up the street, struggling against the flow of angry men that still poured from the houses, heading for the fight.

As we turned the corner we saw Joseph and Tommy still up on the rooftops, hesitating as to which way to turn, where Tin Ghaut Alley leads down to the river.

"No," we bellowed. "Not down there!"

The streets near the alley were quieter, as everyone still milled around the rendezvous.

"Come here!" we cried.

They heard and saw us, relief in their faces.

"Get down! We've somewhere safe to take thee!"

They scrambled down, finding footholds on the rainwater

pipes and at last they were there on the street with us. There was no time for hugging or joy. "We've to get t' your Aunt Hester's," I told Tommy,

We could hear cries and the dull thuds of flying bricks and stones coming from Grape Lane, and as we tore up Kirkgate nobody stopped us or even seemed to notice us.

"Fire it! Fire it!" we heard them shouting.

We burst into Hester's kitchen, making Mam leap up from the settle, spilling warm ale all down her gown.

"Bless thee, Lady Hilda," she whispered, pulling our Joseph into her arms, careless that his breeches were more ragged than ever and he was covered with soot.

"Mam, Mam," Tommy cried, clinging to his mother. Big lad though he was, tears poured down his face, making clean pink trails on his dirty cheeks, as Lyddy hugged him.

I had an urge to hug him too but I was too shy and besides, I knew that there was much more that needed to be done.

Polly felt the same. "We've no time for fussing," she cried.

"No," I tried to speak calmly. "There's a great gang o' Whitby folk broken into the rendezvous!"

"We heard the row," Joseph gasped. "When t' guards went out to see what were up, we took our chance and shot up the chimney and got out on t' roof."

"I can see that," Mam dusted him down, still delighted just to see him.

"Listen!" Polly cried. "There's guns being fired!"

"People going mad," I added. "Tearing The Grapes Hotel apart. They're calling it their Bastille and saying they'll fire it!"

"I knew it . . . bound to happen," Hester shook her head. "But there'll be hell t' pay!"

At last they were listening to us.

"They've done it while most the of the press-gang are out and about their business," I told them. "But what'll happen when they get back tonight?"

Then Hester spoke slowly. "Why lass, if what yer say is true . . . I dread t' think!"

Mam looked at Lyddy. "We ought t' get these lads out o' Whitby fast," she said.

"Aye," Lyddy agreed. "They'd maybe call 'em deserters now! Yer know what that means?"

"They'd shoot us," Joseph went white beneath the dirt on his cheeks.

"Don't y' fret lad," said Hester snatching up her shawl as she spoke. "We have our secret ways o' moving goods and people safely out o' Whitby."

"Should we not wait for darkness?" Lyddy asked.

"Nay," Hester insisted. "That's when the damned press-gang will return, and who knows what'll happen then. We'll go at once."

"Won't we be seen?" I asked.

"Nay! Not the way I'll take thi, honey, and by the sound o' it, the constables will have their hands full enough and not be hunting these fellows just yet."

So without wasting any more time we all set out. Hester looked down Kirkgate and waved us to follow. We walked quickly along to the bottom of the Church Stairs, then turned up the steep donkey path, that curved round and up to the cliffs above. I was surprised at the direction she'd taken, but kept my mouth shut and followed the others. We'd not gone far when she went off to the right, along a small pathway beside a terrace of tiny cottages and down a steep flight of steps. Now I began to understand what Hester meant by secret ways; the path we took wound in and out of yards and gardens, up and down steps and alleyways, but always following a narrow hidden route, with high walls on either side of us.

"It's the free-traders route," I whispered.

Polly nodded and smiled. We seemed to be discovering

quite a bit about smugglers' ways, since our lives had become so frightening. At one point we knocked on a door and marched straight into somebody's kitchen. The woman of the house was just setting out fresh bread to cool on her windowsill.

"Don't mind us, Lizzie?" said Hester. "It's the press-gang!"

"Bless thi," Lizzie told us. "Has tha far t' go?"

"Sandwick and Burning Mountain," Lyddy spoke.

"Here take a loaf, honey," she thrust a cooling bread loaf into my arms. "Tha'd best not stop to seek out food."

There was no time for thanks for quickly and quietly we were out of her side door and again up a long passage, then down another steep flight of narrow steps. On we went, through a fisherman's shed, where the old man stood up without a word from mending his nets and pushed aside the wooden chest that he'd been sitting on. He lifted a trapdoor hidden beneath and we hurried down a strong wooden ladder, arriving in a very long building that smelled of sacking and glue. The building was full of workers who walked steadily back and forth, but nobody stopped their work to question us.

10
A Pope's Curse

I stared about me. This strange shed-like place that we found ourselves in seemed to stretch away into the distance forever.

"The ropery," Tommy whispered and I realised that he was right.

We marched on past the oblivious rope-makers for what seemed ages and at the far end of the building we headed down some cellar steps and into a dark tunnel where we had to feel the walls to stop us stumbling.

"Under the street," Hester whispered.

When we came out again into daylight she was grinning at our amazement. Then came another stretch of narrow pathway with high walls on either side, then up a ladder to a sail-loft built into the hillside. We stepped out from the back of the sail-loft into fresh green woodland, high above the banks of the River Esk. We had somehow managed to pass right through Whitby Town without ever going through any open street.

We gasped with relief as we looked back and saw Whitby in the distance behind us. "Now then, keep heading up river till yer reach Ruswarp Mill," said Hester.

"But that's inland, far away from Burning Mountain!" Mam was puzzled.

"It's not the quickest way." Hester agreed, "I grant yer that, but believe me Mary, it's the safest. Cross the Esk by the bridge at Ruswarp, then over the Carrs and north up Featherbed Lane, on towards Newholm and Dunsley. Tha'll be heading back towards the sea b' then an' making for tha home by way of woods and moors and hidden paths. Tha'll never need to travel by road until ye'r back at Sandwick Bay."

We kissed Hester and thanked her greatly for her help, but she was in a hurry to get back, uncertain of what might be happening in Whitby. We headed off up river, keeping well into the sheltering woods as she'd told us to. Then crossed the Esk at Ruswarp and marched over the low hills that she called the Carrs. We struggled up narrow Featherbed Lane to Aislaby in single file, safe and hidden, though it was steep and made us breathless. I knew then what Hester had meant by hidden paths.

It was growing dark by the time we reached the outskirts of Dunsley village.

"I can't take another step," Polly complained. "And my stomach is crying out for food."

I was glad that she'd said it, for I felt the same, though I didn't like to moan.

"Fair enough," Lyddy agreed, throwing herself down upon the drying bracken that surrounded us. "We'll share the bread and get up our spirits for Lythe Bank, though we'd best keep away from the road and stay in the shelter o' Mulgrave Woods."

"You lads are quiet," said Mam. "Did they feed yer in that place?"

The two lads looked at each other in silence. Joseph shuddered. "A bit o' mouldy bread and disgusting broth," he told us. "Some of 'em wolfed it down, but I couldn't touch a drop. There were fellows as had been there a week in that filthy den."

"How many?" Mam asked, her voice soft with concern.

Tommy shrugged his shoulders. "Mebbe fifty," he said. "The gang were bent on getting a hundred, so we'd heard."

Lyddy nodded. "Hester told me they'd taken her

neighbour Robbie – boarded his whaling ship as it returned and grabbed the whole crew."

"Aye, we were with Robbie," Tommy told us. "He were desperate and wept all night. He'd never got a chance to see his new-born bairn."

There was silence for a moment as we all grieved for Robbie's desperation, then a touch of wicked joy crept into Joseph's voice. "He's out o' there now, though," he said and we all laughed. "He were first up on the rooftops!"

"And I pray he stays out," Lyddy whispered.

Tommy sighed and shuddered. "Can't believe we're free. Thought we'd had it. I've never liked being out beneath the sky as I do tonight."

"But it's getting very dark," I whispered shivering.

"Don't be feared o' that, we'll have a bright moon by the looks of it," Lyddy told me, nudging my elbow. "We're getting close to home now and I know every tiny pathway, for I've done quite a bit o' walking in the moonlight," she patted my face, chuckling. "Now can we have a bite o' that bread my lass?"

"Eh Lyddy," Mam shook her head, laughing. "I never thought tha midnight dashes could come in so useful. Of course, I know nowt of such things!"

Their cheerful fooling made me feel better.

"I could hold yer hand," Tommy offered.

Polly giggled at that.

"Oh could you?" I replied huffily, but secretly I was pleased.

It was early in the morning when we stumbled back to Burning Mountain, giving Father a terrible fright. Lyddy and Tommy came with us and bedded down beside our hearth, for Mam insisted that the lads could not safely stay in their homes for long and that we must plan carefully what to do in the morning.

I was worn out but couldn't stop thinking about what had happened. It had been a dreadful day, but for the moment we seemed to be safe. It hadn't all been bad; I had let Tommy hold my hand as we stumbled uphill through the woods, and his strong warm grip had felt very pleasant to me. I'd been glad that the darkness covered up the big smile that I'd got on my face.

We tried to sleep, but it seemed impossible, despite our exhaustion, so we all got up and sat around our fire while Mam made oakcakes instead.

"I cannot believe they'd shoot these two lads as deserters," Father shook his head.

"If you'd seen that fierce lot that have set up their rendezvous in Whitby, you'd not put anything past them," Mam could not settle her misgivings. "Do *you* think that I wish to send my lad away from his home? I do not, but I want him alive."

Lyddy was deep in thought, listening to the argument that swung between Mam and Dad.

"It's the damned curse," Mam insisted. "Waint go away. A pope's curse is a terrible powerful thing. Mother always warned me not to marry an alum worker. I should ha' married a weaver, that's what she said, then we could spend our days peacefully spinning and weaving together."

Polly and I sighed and exchanged glances. We'd heard this many times before.

"Don't talk so about the curse! It's foolishness!" Dad insisted. "Nowt but a fairy tale."

Dad had never taken much notice of the alum workers' curse, but the thought of it made me shudder. Many of the workers believed doggedly in the thing.

The story went that Sir Thomas Challoner, way back in the time of Queen Elizabeth, had gone off travelling through the countries of Europe and that he'd seen the pope's alum works placed amongst similar rocks and cliffs to the ones that we have here in Yorkshire. The secret of making alum belonged to the Vatican, but Sir Thomas persuaded one of the pope's workers to come away with him, and set up alum works here in Yorkshire. When the pope discovered what had happened, he was said to have laid a terrible curse on all those who meddled with alum.

"Rubbish!" Father insisted. "The pope must ha' been angry," he agreed. "And maybe he excommunicated Sir Thomas, for until our alum workings were set up in Yorkshire, he'd been able to charge whatever he liked for his crystals. But the curse is just superstition. I'll never believe in such things; plain ignorance it is!"

Lyddy suddenly looked up from the fireside and spoke to Mam. "My lad's in danger too Mary and we fisher-folk have no curse on us – not that I know ought about, anyway. Yer can't believe that rubbish?"

"Now who's talking?" said Mam. "Whose husband turns about and goes back home if a woman looks at him when he's walking down to his boat? And if a pig runs across his path . . . well?"

Lyddy had to chuckle then for the fisherman's superstitions were well known. "Aye, tha's got me there, but curse or no curse, pig or no pig, what are we going to do about these lads?"

Suddenly Father got up from the settle and knocked the ash out of his pipe. "I think I might just have an idea," he said. He rushed out of the cottage and was back within moments. "Aye, she's still here! They're loading up *The Primrose*, Captain Camplin's boat. He's bound for the Thames. These lads could be off to London on *The Primrose*, delivering our alum crystals, then come safely back with the urine pipes, when things have cooled down a bit. If there's any trouble, I daresay Captain Camplin would find space for them in the gin-smuggling holes!"

11
The Primrose

There was silence for a moment, then Joseph pulled a disgusted face. "What, go off in a piss-pot?" he cried.

Piss-pots, was the ruder name for the sturdy Whitby-built boats that came and went from Burning Mountain. *The Primrose*, despite her sweet name, did a very heavy job of work, bringing coal from Newcastle, then taking alum crystals down to the Thames and returning with a cargo of Londoners' urine, stored in long barrels that we called pipes. The stench of *The Primrose* cut through the other foul smells of Burning Mountain, and we all knew when the boat had arrived.

Lyddy grinned. "That's fine coming from one who collects the stuff every morning. I'm surprised tha's so delicate."

We said nothing, for we knew how deeply Joseph hated his work.

"That boat might stink, but it could save yer life," Lyddy clearly thought it a good idea.

"Never mind whether it stinks or not," said Mam. "I don't want him going down to the Thames, that's where they take the impressed men. They'd be sailing straight towards danger."

"I'd maybe agree," said Father, "if it were any other than Captain Camplin, but the man's as skilled at his job and as crafty as they come. He'll not let us down. Besides, none of the naval ships down there will recognise our lads. It's this lot up here that we've got to keep them away from."

"Well," said Tommy. "I daresay *The Primrose* would be

better than one of his majesty's ships. And it'd definitely be better than being caught and shot."

"Aye," Joseph agreed glumly.

"Are you going, lads?" Father was agitated. "There's no time left, and I'll have Douthwaite round here in a minute, angry that I'm not there in the boiler house!"

They looked at each other. "Aye," they agreed.

"Then there's not a moment to lose." As they rose to their feet, Father snatched up a strong hempen bag that Mam had made from her own spun threads and pulled down a pair of breeches that were hanging over the fire to dry, thrusting them into the bag.

Mam was on her feet and racing around our house-place, snatching up a knife, a loaf of bread and two earthenware water bottles. "Aye! Aye! It's the best that we can do," she cried. "Captain Camplin will be off as soon as he's loaded; he'll not want to hang about."

Lyddy hovered uncomfortably by the hearth, wanting to help, but uncertain how. "I should fetch things from Sandwick," she fretted.

"Don't worry Lyddy," Mam saw her fears. "There's no time. All that can be taken will be shared with Tommy."

"It will," Joseph agreed.

He was trembling as he took the bag from Mam. He's scared, I thought, and for once I was glad that I wasn't a lad. Then as he turned to kiss me, I saw that he was excited too. "Goodbye to the collecting barrels," he whispered.

Lyddy stayed to watch her son sail away on *The Primrose*, then marched back over the cliff tops to Sandwick Bay. Father went back to his work in the boiler house. At last it seemed that we might have time to draw breath.

"They're safe as they can be now," said Mam. "Safe for a time at least, and now my two fine lasses, yer must take your brother's place and do his work."

Polly and I looked at each other in horror. We hadn't thought of this.

"Oh yes," Mam insisted. "Joseph's job must be done in the morning and gather a bit o' seaweed in the afternoon. Urine pays better than seaweed and until your father finds the best way o' using kelp, urine has to be collected same as ever. Now then, fetch the mule and set off at once. The other collectors are at their work already."

Just for a moment I'd have risked anything to have our Joseph back.

Polly wrinkled her nose. "I wish I were a lad. It should've been me that went sailing away over the sea."

"Not where they're going," Mam told her firmly. "Captain Camplin'll make them work their way, I've no doubt o' that. Now come on, off yer go!"

"Why can't Father use kelp?" I muttered. "Other works do!"

"Aye, and they keep their secrets to thissens!" Mam growled.

So we walked round to the stables to find Patience the mule, the most bad-tempered, awkward beast on earth.

"You can strap the barrels on," I told Polly.

"I'm not. You're the oldest. You do it!"

I sighed. "We'll do it together," I said.

The days that followed were packed with distasteful work. Collecting urine from cottage doorsteps was not a job that we relished any more than Joseph did; we'd rather face the back-breaking seaweed-gathering all day, though it seemed that now we must do both.

"Can't we do wi'out collecting for a while?" we begged that night, as we sat in front of the fire exhausted.

Father shook his head, wrinkling his brow with worry. "We shall have urine shortages soon. One thing leads to another,

54

I've seen it all happen before. The press-gang take seamen off the boats, then all sea traffic slows down, and our stocks of raw materials run low. Thank goodness that we've plenty o' coal for the time being. If the press-gang move north, troubling folk in Newcastle, the next thing will be coal shortages."

I sighed.

"Nay, we need every drop of local urine we can get. Saltwick and Peak Works are taking what they can in Whitby, I hear they've set collecting barrels in the streets."

"Aye," we nodded. We knew only too well how true that was.

Father drew a hand across his brow and sighed. "Sir Rupert owes us three months wages and isn't like to put things right very fast at this rate. He complains about the war and shortages and says that we must somehow keep production up. All he sent down as payment last week was two fleeces. You knows what that means."

"We know, Father," we both replied.

My shoulders drooped at the thought of it. It meant that Mam must spend her daylight hours washing and combing and spinning wool, before we could take it to sell on to the dyers up the River Esk.

Still, I hated to see Father so fretful and anxious. "Don't fear," I told him, kissing the deep folds in his brow. "We'll get the stinking stuff for yer."

We knew that there was good reason to worry; the market for alum could be very uncertain. Father had often told us about the terrible time when he and his brother Robert were lads. The price of alum had dropped very low and the Alum Master paid his workers with produce instead of money.

"I wouldn't have minded so much," he'd say, "but most of the stuff was old and beginning to rot, so me and Robert were sent off to market with a cart full o' rotting turnips and sprouting grain. We ended up almost giving it away and earning nowt. Rotting turnips don't sell easy," he'd shake his head, remembering. "We worked and worked and we damn near starved."

It seemed to us those desperate times might be returning. In recent years the workers had begun to set up their little gardens and cultivated vegetable plots. Father insisted that there'd been many a time that the rows of kale and cabbages had saved our lives.

As summer passed and the weather chilled a little Father became very busy each evening, carefully gathering seeds from the few vegetable plants that he'd allowed to flower and go to seed. He dug over new patches of earth to extend our garden and planted extra rows of cabbages and kale, for as he said, "It's better to prepare for the worst in uncertain times like these."

12

The Collecting Ladies

So as the weeks passed, Polly and I gritted our teeth and fought over which of us was to lead the mule and who should collect the jugs. We both thought collecting the worse job, for it meant carrying the jugs and pouring out the contents, which slopped on to our clothes if we didn't pour carefully enough, or if Patience moved, as she usually did. There wasn't much to choose between the jobs though, for the mule driver would often get bruised shins from Patience's kicking, as well as a soaked apron.

"I really know now how Joseph felt," I said.

"Aye," Polly sighed. Though we still squabbled, for the most part we were better friends, struggling over the cliff-tops together with our smelly load.

Father praised us for our efforts and called us the Collecting Ladies.

"Lady Poll and Lady Nan," we giggled.

It was while we were collecting from Sandwick Top Green that we heard from Parson Eardy that the rendezvous in Whitby had been destroyed.

"Almost gutted," he told us. "The militia's been brought in to keep the peace and an enquiry set up. Oh yes, Whitby's full of soldiers and it seems they'll stay a while. The press-gang's moved on to Newcastle to try their luck there, but I heard than an elderly farmer's been arrested, charged with aiding and abetting rebellion."

"Old William?" I whispered.

Polly dug me sharply in the ribs lest I gave more away than I should, but the parson took no notice and shook his head sadly. "I cannot see how one old man can be responsible for that," he murmured. "It's more that somebody must get the blame and be used as an example."

Feeling his guarded sympathy, I dared to ask the parson more. "Did all the impressed fellows get away, sir?"

"I believe they did, my dear," he nodded.

I sighed with relief for poor Robbie and his wife.

"And I hear," the parson carried on, smiling meaningfully. "I hear that some of them have chosen to voyage in a different direction," he winked. "I keep such fellows in my prayers," he nodded piously.

"Even the parson hates the press-gang," I whispered as Polly and I stumbled away down the track.

As late summer turned to autumn, Polly and I struggled hard to do Joseph's job, but Mam was always ready with a good warming stew of vegetables after we returned at noon with full barrels. More often than not it had a taste of fish to it if Lyddy had sent over one of the younger Welfords with a parcel of fish tails.

Mam let us sit by the fire with our feet up while she spun one spindle of washed sheep's wool.

"Keeping spinning! Keep spinning, Mam!" we'd beg, but as soon as that spindle was empty, the wheel would stop and she'd turn aside from her work to lift our kelp baskets from the wall nails.

"Off you go again!" she'd cry, shooing us off down the steep cliff path with our baskets on our backs.

All afternoon we gathered the seaweed that we call tangles and carried it to Annie, who spread it out to dry in the kelp hut. She'd burn it carefully once it was dry enough and collect the ashes to make the kelp lees for Father to try his experiments with.

We grubbed about, slipping and sliding on the rocks, our baskets growing heavier at each handful of tangles that we added. As we gathered we often glanced out to sea, hoping to see the familiar shape of *The Primrose* on the horizon, returning with her cargo, but we looked in vain. We worked until the light began to fade, then stumbled back up the cliff path, desperate for warm porridge and the mattress that we shared.

On Sundays we went to the chapel near Sandwick Bay Top Green, then after our dinner we helped Father with the vegetable plot. That was the best time of the week, digging and planting and Father in a good humour, with fine full bellies for once.

We heard nothing from Joseph and Tommy, but Father said that was a good sign, for Captain Camplin would certainly let us know if they'd fallen foul of the Admiralty.

Sad news came from Whitby; old William was convicted of aiding and abetting rebellion. He'd been taken off to York, a condemned man, due to be hanged at Micklegate Tyburn. There was a great deal of distress and crying "shame" about it, for William was seventy years of age and much respected, though it was also whispered that he'd been a wild rebellious fellow in his youth.

Lyddy came up the cliff path to Burning Mountain to tell us of his death. "It's strange," she said, "but somehow there's relief in it. They say he died in the prison cart and when they opened it up at York to get him out, all they found was a peaceful corpse."

"Aye," Mam agreed, wiping sudden tears away with the back of her hand. "It *is* better that he died before they could hang him."

Lyddy chuckled, her arms folded tight across her chest. "Trust William – he got the better of them in the end."

* * *

Weeks of steady rain made us more miserable than ever, for work must go on at the alum works, rain or not. Everything was harder and more uncomfortable. The jugs of urine must be kept covered, for the stinking stuff must not be diluted at any cost.

"As I often reminded our Joseph," Father told us as he sat beside the fire in the evening, smoking his pipe. "You must be sharp when collecting. The poorer folk will use every trick in the book to make their piss seem more. They'll try diluting it with sea water, just to get their penny at the end o' the month."

"But how can we know?" we asked him.

He shrugged his shoulders. "You must get a sense of it," he insisted. "And watch your suppliers closely; the twitch of tha mouth, the blushing cheek. You cannot tell by looking or smelling but we can tell soon enough when the stuff is poured into the alum liquor."

"Why?" Polly asked. "What happens?"

"Not a damned thing!" he told us thumping his fist down upon the wooden arm of the settle, while Mam clicked her tongue and shook her head as she turned the spinning wheel. "If they've been diluting their urine and deceiving us – not a thing happens when it's poured into the alum liquor. If it's good strong stuff it makes the liquor fizz like yeast put to sugar."

Mam shook her head. "You'd think he loved the stuff," she chuckled and sighed.

Father spoke with pride. "We possess the secrets of alum making, handing it down through our families, and besides it makes us money."

"Sometimes," Mam quickly butted it.

We'd smile when Father started talking like this, but I did understand a little of how he felt. Though we hated the smelly process of making alum, we loved to go into the sheds to watch when the men were breaking open the wooden barrels of finished crystals. As they lifted off the truss hoops and stripped away the wooden staves, crystals came tumbling out sparkling and true, white as snow. That moment was always magical; you couldn't believe that anything so pure and bright could come from greasy shale and piss.

13
Such a Night

The riverbanks flooded as the rain continued, but then one morning early in October we woke to sharp, bright sunshine, the rain had ceased. Suddenly the world seemed to be a wonderful place once again, for Father returned home at noon with a huge beaming smile on his face.

"The London stage has brought news o' *The Primrose*," he cried. "She's gained the best prices in the market – the only alum boat that's got through with a full cargo o' crystals to sell. Douthwaite tells us that Sir Rupert has promised to pay all he owes."

Mam couldn't believe it. "It's an ill wind," she said. "The press-gang seems to have done us some good. They've stopped other alum boats getting through and we are the winners in that war."

"Aye, it's all mad," said Father. "The world is going mad but we'd best be grateful for small mercies."

"I'd rather have my lad back home," Mam whispered.

It seemed that the press-gang's activities had brought many of the other alum works to a standstill and so the London prices paid for our goods had really shot up.

"Things are looking bright," Father insisted. "There's to be a fine meal to celebrate our good fortune, with meat and ale provided by Sir Rupert. Look at me, Mary," he said, grabbing Mam round the waist and making us giggle. "Now who says now that we're cursed?"

"When is this meal to be?" Polly bellowed.

"At once! Today! For a change, Sir Rupert's full of praise for his manager and his workers. We've kept up production whilst others slumped. So work is stopping and we're to be rewarded."

"Oh," Mam sighed, her cheeks pink with pleasure. "If only our Joseph were here, then all would be well."

"Never mind what can't be helped," Father told her, kissing her forehead. "Get making some of your famous oatcakes – and lasses, will yer clean carrots and potatoes for the pot? Sir Rupert is supplying us with roast beef, mutton and barley ale. I've got to get back to the boiler house now, for there's much to be done if we're to leave the pans later."

None of us needed telling twice, such good news travelled fast. The pickmen and barrowmen came home early. The clang of Bart Little's hammer ceased and he came out from his smithy wiping grime from his face and hands. The coopers set half-made barrels aside. Father and the other housemen were the last to leave their work, for the coal fires beneath the boiling pans were to be dampened down for once and couldn't be left for long. I couldn't remember another time when work had ceased in daylight hours. Even the seaweed gatherers were called up from the beach.

Workers and their families rushed excitedly from cottage to cottage, delighted with their good fortune. Trestles and tables were dragged outside into the bright October sunshine and wooden settles, stools and benches fixed up all about. The littlest children were sent up the cliff-side to stand by the spoil heaps, ready to give warning when they saw the food arriving.

A good smell of fresh-made oatcakes, roasting potatoes and vegetables came from every open door. At last the sound of distant clapping and cheers from the lookouts, told us that they'd spied a great train of servants coming down from Whingate Hall. Sir Rupert and his lady carried in sedan chairs headed the procession. The butler and four cellar-men walked beside them, stumbling downhill, bearing huge flagons of ale. The procession moved slowly but steadily, wending its way down past the steadily burning clamps and the steeping-pits, towards Alum Row, on the lower cliff ledge.

The workers came from their doorways with hot bowls of cooked vegetables in their arms and the few scraps of cutlery that they possessed. We all took our places at the tables, cheering wildly as great platters of meat were placed before us.

Sir Rupert and his lady stayed just long enough to receive our grateful thanks and to see mugs raised to them. They invited Mr Douthwaite to go back to the hall to dine with them. He accepted readily, his face flushed with the honour. The Master of Whingate and his wife stepped back into their sedan chairs and returned to their home on the cliff top, waving graciously from the windows, carried by four strong stable lads, rather red in the face. Mr Douthwaite walked behind them, used to making the trail up the steep cliff-side. The servants soon followed while we hungry workers gave all our attention to the delicious food, politeness forgotten.

The meat was tender and well cooked, with jugs of rich gravy to accompany it. We ate and drank with relish, for we'd all suffered empty bellies in recent weeks, whilst we'd worked harder than we'd ever done before.

"God bless Sir Rupert!" Annie cried, waving her mug in the air.

"God bless Old Rupe!" we cheered, clattering our wooden mugs together, full of sudden charity to the master who'd left us hungry and unpaid for months. It was just at that moment that we heard a gentle rumbling above us coming from the cliff tops and suddenly the table shook, knocking over mugs and spilling ale. Three of the cottage doors on Alum Row slammed shut, one after the other, then all went quiet for a moment.

"What was that?" Polly asked.

I looked up towards the spoil heaps and burning clamps that loomed above us.

"Just a bit o' shale," Father told us. "Just a bit o' spent shale slipping down from the heaps, as it often does."

"More than likely," Mam nodded.

"Don't fret Mary," Annie told her. "Hold up yer mug for me to fill again. We must make the most o' this night. Who knows when such a feast may come again."

So the feast went on until the sun began to sink down behind Burning Mountain, so that we could no longer see clearly the big dark shapes of the clamps set in the open quarry above us. We sat there with our bellies full to bursting, I couldn't remember ever feeling so full before.

"Come on our Henry, bring out that fiddle," Annie cried, and when we all begged him, Henry did fetch his fiddle and started to play for us.

A cool breeze sprang up as Annie started to sing, and everyone clapped to keep warm while Polly and me got up to dance. Though my stomach was still full, the more I danced the more I seemed to shake the food down and feel comfortable again. The faster Henry played the faster we danced, swinging our patched skirts about and stamping our clogged feet on the trampled shale that formed the ledge on which our little hovels perched.

Polly shrieked with excitement as we tottered back and forth, then all of a sudden we fell over, rolling together wild with laughter on the floor.

"This ground's moving," Polly gulped and giggled.

"Far too much ale for a little lass," Father told her.

I pulled her to her feet, though I seemed to feel giddy enough myself. We stumbled back to our places as everyone clapped and cheered us.

"Now Mary," Annie cried. "Give us a song. We want to hear that fine voice o' yours! Come on!"

So Mam got up to sing a song that we'd loved when we were small. A song deeply linked with the place that we called home.

> *Whin bush, whin bush,*
> *Bloom on Easter Day,*
> *Paint our eggs all golden,*
> *To roll along the way.*
>
> *Whin bush, whin bush,*
> *Sweetly bloom through May,*
> *Fill our hives with honey,*
> *To eat in summer hay.*
>
> *Whin bush, whin bush,*
> *Burn for us today,*
> *Black sticks, black sticks,*
> *Burn our shale away.*
>
> *Whin bush, whin bush,*
> *All winter, green you stay,*
> *Feed our goats and feed our cows,*
> *Right through to Easter Day.*

There was happiness all about us, but I glanced up and caught my father straining his neck, distracted from Mam's deep pleasant voice. He was looking anxiously towards the clamps and spoil heaps above us, then when another, louder rumbling sound came he was up and out of his seat in an instant.

Mam stopped her song. "What is it?" she cried, as the feasters fell silent.

"Second clamp at Ridge Top," Father told her. "It moved! I swear it moved!"

There were gasps, but nobody spoke or cried out – faces

were full of disbelief that Father should cause panic at such a wonderful feast. We were used to small landslides, living up there on the cliff ledges, with the sea battering at our feet, we couldn't expect anything else.

Bart Little rose from the table and went quickly to stand beside Father. He was a tough, strong fellow, but we all knew that he'd got a horror of landslides, ever since he'd lost his family in one as a small lad. He rubbed his hands together fretfully, staring up into the gloom above.

Henry tucked his fiddle under his arm and went to join them. "I'd say y're right, Thomas," he agreed, his voice hushed and a little shaky. "See where yon clamp is glowing red, I'd swear it's breaking up. We'd best take a gang o' fellows and go up t' see if we can steady it? Where's Douthwaite, when you need him?"

"Aye," Father agreed. "We don't want that lot tumbling down on us!" He looked quickly about, and seemed to take charge, nodding his head at certain men who rose at once from their seats and went to him. "Don't fear," Father told us, his voice calm enough now to reassure us a little. "Best clear away our feast – light's gone anyway now. Fetch lanterns can you, Henry?"

"Aye." There were murmurs of agreement and as the men set off to climb the steep slope, we busied ourselves collecting up our precious knives, forks and wooden trenchers. We dragged stools and benches back to our homes.

14
Are We Cursed?

As I hauled two stools back into our house-place I heard another rumble, heavier still, and swore that the very ground beneath my feet gave a shiver. Sharp wrenching, cracking sounds made me drop both the stools in fright and stare about me until I saw a jagged break that had appeared in the timbers of our cottage door posts. I ducked my head and ran straight outside, hearing it creak as I passed. Everyone was staring up through the fading light, towards the top of Burning Mountain once more.

"God help us," Annie cried. "That top clamp *is* going and the next!"

Now there were cries of deep distress and alarm as we saw that she was right. The whole clamp toppled sideways as we watched, its burning centre glowing red as it broke apart, thick white smoke belching from its belly and rolling down the hillside towards us.

"Cursed! Cursed!" Annie cried.

"Aye this is it! This is our curse dear God!"

"What shall happen to us?"

Desperate shrieks went up and my heart started thundering loudly as I felt the ground move again beneath our feet. Lanterns bobbed wildly about in the distance telling us that the men were running back, slithering and sliding down the path, as the clamps began one by one to topple and fall. Another great thundering tremor brought the dark mass of spoil heaps shifting down the hillside in our direction.

There was panic, people ran into their houses to snatch up their most treasured possessions; then, as cracks appeared in their walls they ran out again, screaming and grabbing at their children. Where could we go? We could not go upwards, we could not run towards Sandwick for the whole cliff-side was falling, and beneath us there was nothing but the freezing North Sea.

Father came pelting back to us, the other men following, frantically seeking their wives and children. I'd never seen Father look so frightened and bewildered.

"Where can we go?"

"What can we do?"

Polly grabbed my arm, pinching me so tight that it hurt. "We're going to die," she gulped.

"Hush!" I cried, hugging her tightly. Then with a terrible cracking, wrenching sound, the wall of the boiler house caved in, sinking straight down into a pit that appeared in the crumbling ground. There was a great thundering bang as the leaden boiling pans tipped and alum liquor, still hot, came flooding out through gaping holes in the side of the building. Braying and thumping came from the stables, and one mule broke loose and crashed past us up towards the tumbling spoil heaps.

"Get out o' the way! Shift thissens!"

The boiler house roof came crashing down.

"All's going," Mam cried. "Everything! We're cursed – we'll die!"

We moved instinctively towards the edge of the lower cliff away from all the terror above us. But it seemed that there was no escape for the ground by the cliff-edge began to give. Father grabbed hold of both Polly and me, hugging us tightly to him, trying somehow to comfort us. I shut my eyes, waiting to die. But suddenly I felt Father breath more freely. "Thank God! Thank God!" he whispered.

"What is it?" I asked.

Father laughed. I thought he'd gone mad with fear.

He laughed again and drew us stumbling and sliding further on towards the sinking edge of our cliff ledge. I still kept my eyes tight shut, for I did not want to see what lay below us.

"No, Father! No!" we cried, thinking that maybe he was going to throw us over into the sea, thinking that might be a more merciful death.

But Father kissed us both, his arms clasped tight about our waists. "We are not cursed!" he shouted cheerfully. "We're not going to die! Open your eyes my lasses and see your salvation."

And when I did at last dare to open my eyes, tears of joy flooded them, spilling down my cheeks. There beneath us, with oil lamps lit, gleaming golden in the dusk was *The Primrose* nosing her way towards us through the narrow rocky cut in the scar that acted as a dock.

Never was the sight of a boat more welcome.

"This way," Father shouted back to the others. "*The Primrose*! Follow us down to the sea."

"*The Primrose*! We're saved!" The cry went up from all those behind us.

Suddenly we were all tottering towards the crumbling cliff edge, feet clogged with mud, grasping at bushes and handfuls of grass and earth. But we were not so fearful now, for although the path and steps were gone at least as the damp earth slid beneath our feet it carried us down towards the safety of *The Primrose*.

Captain Camplin dropped anchor out where the water was still deep. He stood on deck, shouting out sharp orders while his crew ran fore and aft, hauling on ropes, bringing down the sails.

"No nearer!" he shouted. "No nearer!"

The small boats that we kept at the dockside had vanished beneath growing piles of rock and shale. There was nothing for it but to go wading out into the freezing foam while ropes and ladders were thrown down from the deck. The two small rowing boats were lowered, but they could only take a few of us. I lost Polly then, though I could hear her shouting my name. I rushed into the sea along with the others, and fell stumbling on the slippery scar. I'd lost both my clogs. Soaked and gasping, with a mouthful of seawater, for a few moments I thought this means of rescue worse than death, but Father's arms went round me and hauled me up again.

"Polly!" I cried. "Where's Polly?"

"She's here," Father bellowed. "Just behind. Mam's got her."

And then I was reassured by Polly's clutching hands.

"You must climb!" Father told us, putting one of the ship's ropes into my hands.

"I can't," I cried. My hands were numb and I could do nothing but shiver and shake.

"Climb or die!" Father's voice was urgent. Then he spoke low and calm. "You can do it lass, Polly follows close behind, hold tight and climb! Don't slip back, you'll crush your sister."

Then I knew that I must somehow find the strength and slowly, step by step, shuddering and clinging tightly, I began to shin up the rope, pressing my bare wet feet into the thick rough coil, then against the side of *The Primrose*.

At last a strong hand above caught my apron straps and hauled me bodily upwards and I went scrambling over the side of the gunwales. I thought that a quick and smacking kiss landed on my cheek as I staggered about the decking, stunned. I couldn't see properly and thought that I must be dreaming, for whoever had hauled me up and kissed me so fast had vanished.

"Nan!" I heard Polly's desperate cry and went back at once to the gunwales. Polly's drenched, white face appeared, and I saw that it was Joseph that was heaving her up and over the edge. I grabbed her arm to help, and Joseph turned to me with another quick kiss.

"All right," I said. "Tha's kissed me once."

"Nay," he frowned. "Take Polly and try to warm each other!" he told us, his voice full of authority.

I saw Henry Knaggs hauled aboard, his precious fiddle tucked under his arm and the bow clenched tight between his teeth. I shuddered as he fell on to the deck, dragging his left leg, groaning with pain but still gripping on to his fiddle. His mother followed but as soon as she staggered on to the deck she pulled off her shawl, wrapping it about Henry's shoulders.

"Come away," I told Polly. "We'd best do as Joseph says, and try to get warm."

Mam followed us and we were all soon huddled together beneath a woollen rug that Captain Camplin had taken from his own bunk. When at last every one of the alum workers was hauled aboard all cries subsided and a grateful quietness seemed to spread amongst us. We were battered and bruised, with nasty cuts and wrenched muscles, freezing cold and wet, but we were alive.

Captain Camplin ordered the anchor to be raised and *The Primrose* was poled away from the rocks. "We must be off into deeper sea roads," he told us. "If we wait a moment more we'll be stuck fast in shallow water; trapped beneath the muck that's coming down."

He suggested that we go below decks to find better warmth, offering the use of his own cabin, but though we were freezing cold, we could not take our eyes from the dark moving land that was all that was left of our homes. High on the cliff top we could see the lights of Whingate Hall. The stone wall that edged Sir Rupert's gardens seemed to be ablaze with moving lanterns. Sir Rupert and his family and servants must be up there gazing down on the destruction of Burning Mountain.

"Aye, Douthwaite has done well to be up there!" Annie snarled.

"I don't know," Mam shook her head. "Is Whingate Hall coming down as well?"

We stared into the darkness, but couldn't see anything clearly. We knew that the coal yard had vanished, along with the boiler house, and the tun house and warehouse, our cottages had tumbled down too. The alum channels and the steeping-pits must surely all be broken and destroyed. How could we ever work there again?

Again the whispering began. "Cursed – we're cursed, and always shall be."

But Father wouldn't have it. "Stop that!" he cried. "We'd be a damned sight more cursed without *The Primrose*," he insisted. "Go below deck now. Get warm. Thank Captain Camplin for your lives!"

Father seemed to have taken on Mr Douthwaite's role in his absence, and everyone quietly obeyed his orders.

15
Captain of a Piss-pot!

Captain Camplin took *The Primrose* out to sea, the sails carrying us along fast with a westerly wind behind us – that had added to the havoc on land, but now helped us along nicely. We huddled together dazed and shivering. The crew of the sturdy alum boat cheered us with their rough kindness. A steaming mug of broth was thrust beneath my nose.

I shook my head. "Not hungry," I muttered.

"No, but cold," a familiar voice answered. "It'll warm thee up – get supping!"

I looked up to find Tommy Welford hovering over me dragging a great iron stew pot in one hand, ladle and mug in the other. He looked older and somehow more of a man.

I was so glad to see him there, looking so strong and at home aboard the alum boat.

The ladle clanged down on to the floor as he bent to kiss my cheek. "There's another kiss," he whispered. "Don't fret. Y're safe now."

"Another kiss?" I asked. Then I realised that it must have been Tommy who'd hauled me over the gunwales and on to *The Primrose*. "Was it you pulled me aboard?"

"Aye," he nodded. "I had to see thee safe, didn't I?"

I smiled up at him, forgetting that my hair and face were filthy.

"Give us a sup o' that broth," Mam butted in. "Bart here can't stop shaking, and Henry needs warming too." Tommy turned away from me to serve the other frozen folk.

We spent a cold choppy night out at sea, with the sails down and *The Primrose* hovering in the Whitby sea roads. Nobody could sleep.

"Well I never thought I'd be so glad to see the Captain of a piss-pot!" Annie insisted, making us all laugh at last.

"I never thought I'd be so glad to get aboard a piss-pot!" Mam agreed.

It was only then, that I realised that, though the boat must stink to high heaven, I'd not given it a thought.

"Why it doesn't seem to smell so bad," I murmured.

"Y're right lassie," Annie cried, breathing in deeply. "I must say, I'd have married the captain myself, if I'd known his boat'd smell so nice!"

Annie made fun of Captain Camplin all through the night, and would not allow us to weep; she even made Henry laugh and curse her by telling him to play us a jig. Then early in the morning, as the tide filled up the harbour, we sailed into Whitby Town.

There was quite a crowd there to meet us, for the news of our disaster had travelled fast. Mr Douthwaite was there, along with Sir Rupert who looked white-faced and worried. They talked low-voiced with Father and Captain Camplin, all four men shaking their heads. I almost felt sorry for Sir Rupert just for a moment, but then I remembered how hungry we'd been in the last few months and the great jellies and pastries that I'd glimpsed in his kitchen.

Mam clearly felt the same. "And what help is he offering?" she growled to Annie.

Father came back to us, his face drawn. Whingate Hall gardens have collapsed," he told us. "He and his servants fled over the cliff tops. They don't know whether the house is stable and they're fearful to return. He's sent his wife and daughters off in a carriage to Pickering where his sister lives."

"He's not suffering like us!" Mam insisted, her chin

trembling. "He's got the means to see his family safe and comfortable."

"Now then, Mary!" Lyddy Welford came pushing through the crowd to reach us and flung a warm shawl round Mam's shoulders and gave her a good hug.

"Lyddy," Mam was suddenly tearful. "How are you here?"

"I walked all night," she said. "We spied *The Primrose* from Sandwick Bay, and we just stood there helpless, watching Burning Mountain fall," she choked on her words and shook her head.

"Bless thee for coming," Mam whispered.

Lyddy turned to hug us girls. "Have you seen our Tommy?" she asked.

"Aye," I told her. "He's fine and well and looks like – a man!"

Lyddy smiled and kissed my dirty cheek.

We must have made a sad sight as we were stood there in a forlorn group on St Anne's Staith. Our patched clothes were now in shreds, barely decent and caked in thick mud. My feet were bare, so cold and numb at least they didn't hurt much. Our hair was matted with mud that began to set hard as it dried. Most of us could only hobble slowly about, so many bad bruises and wrenched ankles were there. I could see that we were lucky compared to poor Henry who bit his lip, refusing to make a sound, though his cheeks were deathly white and he grimaced at every movement.

Polly clutched my arm. "I want to be clean," she whimpered. "I want to be clean."

Lyddy found Tommy at last and admired his strong seaman's breeches and woollen hat, but it was then that the full meaning of our loss began to sink in. We had lost everything, our home, our beds, our cooking pots and our Sunday clothes. We'd lost our hens and goats and even the pack mules. These filthy rags that barely covered us were all that we'd got. There was nothing to change into. Would we have to spend the rest of our lives in these foul clothes?

Then suddenly Lyddy saw our distress and understood. "Come back wi' me to Sandwick," she said.

"Y've not got room," Mam shook her head.

"I've been trying hard to think all night," Father said. "My brother Robert would help us, I'm sure he would. But it'll take time to get a message to Peak. If we went there I could help him with his work and maybe find a way to pay him back. I thank you most kindly Lyddy, but we know nowt o' fishing life. We're better to go to another alum works if we can."

Lyddy nodded her understanding.

"Aye," Mam agreed. "But where do we go today?"

"Today tha comes to me." It was Hester Welford speaking. She stood there behind us on the quayside, fish basket on her head and the other hand on her hip. She looked so determined that just the sight of her made me feel better.

"Oh Hester," Mam hesitated. "Y've helped us enough already."

But Hester would not have any argument about it. "Sin' that day when the press-gang took thy lads, Whitby is a different place. Thy lads' misfortune brought all t' trouble to a head. Oh aye, we've soldiers marching about keeping us in order now, but the press-gang has been moved on and our yards are full of work and whaling men again. You come wi' me, now. We'll make on it's wash day and we'll get thee feeling fit and fine again."

Joseph and Tommy insisted that they stay with Captain Camplin, for there were errands to run and much to do. With the collapse of Burning Mountain the Captain had lost his buyer for the cargo of urine, so he must look about fast to see if he could find another market for the stuff.

Father went to find the Scarborough Carter and beg him to take a message to his brother at Peak alum works.

Whalebone Scrapers

We lasses and Mam set of stiff-legged to follow Lyddy and Hester over the bridge. As we crossed and looked up the river, we could see that what she'd said was true. Whitby was a different place from last time. The yards were full of workers from the Greenland Fishery, cutting up blubber, scraping whalebones and pressing oil. Cheerfully and openly going about their work, though the stink that came from their yards was almost as bad as our alum works.

We followed Hester back to Welfords Yard. Her three daughters were just setting off to the scar, with their wooden pails and baskets, for the daily round of bait-gathering.

"Eeh bless 'em!" they murmured, greatly concerned when they saw the state of us. "How'll they ever get thissens clean?"

"It'll be done!" Hester told them firmly. "I'll not come flither-picking today, nor Alice. She can stay and help."

"Oh thank you, Mam!" Hester's youngest daughter cried, flinging her basket down in a corner of the yard.

"Tha'd best not be thanking me so soon," Hester smiled. "It's like to be harder work than any bait gathering, I'd think."

Hester served us out there in the yard with warming porridge, which we ate with relish. While we ate she pulled out a wooden tub and little Alice ran back and forth to the pump, fetching buckets of water until it was half-filled. Rachel, a skinny old woman who lived across the yard, brought out a second tub for us to use.

"Now then, drop tha poor clothes into t' tub," she told us, pointing a gnarled finger at our rags. She also brought out her ash pot and sprinkled handfuls of white wood ash into the clothes tub. "That'll mebbe help loosen t'muck."

I began to wonder how our rags could be washed without us being left stark naked, when Hester pulled a wooden screen out into the yard from her house-place.

"Have we to stand naked behind that?" Polly whispered.

"Just while tha gets washed," Hester told us. "Once tha's clean I'll fetch out our lass's Sunday petticoats and shawls for thee."

Letting us wear their best clothes was a big sacrifice; Sunday clothes were treasured beyond all.

Hester topped up the wash tub with a bit of hot water from the kettle that bubbled constantly on the reckon above her fire.

"Now then," she asked. "Wha's first?"

We hesitated for it was terrible standing out there in the yard with thick mud slowly drying and chafing all over us. I was desperate to be rid of it, though I didn't relish stripping off either.

"Lasses first," said Mam.

"No, you Mam!"

"Water's getting chilled!" Hester complained.

Mam didn't wait around then. She stripped her top half off boldly and set to washing down her hands and face in the tub. "Warm," she smiled, then she ducked her head in, hair and all, while Hannah and Lyddy stood by with a soft drying cloth and warm rugs to wrap us in.

"Come on, lasses," Lyddy encouraged. "Once tha's clean, Hester'll let thee go inside."

16
In Sad Need of Repair

At last we were all washed and dressed, our hair steaming gently as we sat around Hester's fire. We felt better but still whispered fearfully, wondering what was to become of us. We dozed a little, for the fire made us sleepy, remembering that we'd had no rest at all the night before.

Hester, Lyddy and Alice had gone down to Tate Hill Sands with our dirty clothes in their wash tubs, wooden beetles tucked under their arms. The two women returned at noon.

"Thank goodness the rain's holding off," Lyddy cried. "Eeh, yer ought t'see thy gowns and petticoats, they're scrubbed and beaten clean and all stretched out on Tate Hill Sands t' dry. We've left Alice there to mind 'em."

"Is there ought left of 'em?" Mam asked doubtfully. "They've been darned to death already."

"Now then, don't you worry," Rachel told her. "Though they're in sad need o' repair I've used m' needle and thread to fix up worse clothing than what's out there on t' sands and I've a fine sack o' patches under my bed."

"But we can't pay thee – though we do have money owing to us."

"Nay – I don't want pay," Rachel told her firmly, then added wickedly, "Mind a parcel o' alum crystals to fix my dyes 'ud be a grand reward."

Mum's face crumpled up and I could tell that she was swallowing back tears. "So kind," she muttered. "Everyone's so kind. You'll get yer alum crystals, make no mistake; my brother-in-law will fetch some from Peak, even if we never *do* get them from Burning Mountain again."

We were lucky that the sun came out quite bright that morning, and Alice returned soon after noon with her arms piled high with torn but dry clothes. After a good dinner of oatcakes and bloaters, all the women settled around the fire with needles and threads, and a basket of cloth patches, ready to tackle the tricky job of stitching our rags together again.

Suddenly the yard became full of voices and bustle and the smell of fish as the two older girls returned from their bait-gathering.

"This is summat!" Dolly bellowed. "A little alum lass in my best petticoat and clogs!"

But when I started to unfasten it, she hugged me and swore that she was teasing. They ate their dinner then set about fetching knives and buckets of water to shell the bait and fix up their dad's fishing lines. They shouted and laughed and shoved us about, as we got in their way.

"I tell yer what," said Hester. "Alice, leave the line-bating be. I need a few errands fetching. Take these poor lasses and let them have a little wander round t' town."

Alice grinned at us. "Tha' best come every day," she told us, then added hurriedly, "though I wouldn't wish yer such ill fortune again."

We were glad to get ourselves moving, though I was shocked to find that my shoulder and back ached so badly. I could only hobble on my bashed ankle.

"Aye," said Mam, stitching fast as she always did. "Keeping moving's best thing."

So we limped down Kirkgate to the market place, each with a basket on our arm. Whitby was a lively place, much more so than the last fearful visit that we'd made. The stink of smoked fish and boiled whale blubber was everywhere and the shipyards were full of carpenters sawing and hammering like mad. The market was crammed with farmers and their wives, who'd brought fresh produce into Whitby to sell. A few soldiers paraded through the streets, rifles at the ready. They smiled at the pink-cheeked fisher lasses, seeming rather pleased to be there in Whitby keeping the peace and not down in the southern part of the country, preparing to fight the French.

We headed for Maggie's fish stall to tell her what had happened to us.

"Bless yer honey," she said putting crab claws into our hands. "Haven't yer had troubles enough. I always say t'never rains but it pours!"

We returned with our baskets full and found that Father was back, sitting by Hester's fire. He was washed and pink-cheeked and wearing a worn blue fisherman's smock and breeches.

"What's happening, Father?" I asked.

For all his improved appearance he still looked very drawn and worried.

He smiled then. "We'll manage sweetheart. Somehow we shall manage."

"Will Uncle Robert help us?"

"I'm sure he will, but it looks as though we'd best take a chance and travel on to Peak works, whether he will or not."

Mam was rushing about with hot irons and we could see at once that the women had done a grand job with our clothes. My petticoat was patched with faded pink cotton, my pinafore with blue. They'd managed to scrape together enough patches that matched, so that they almost looked good as new.

"Quickly now," Mam cried. "Change back into your clothes. We must catch *The Primrose* again, before the tide changes."

"What?" we cried. "Are we off again?"

"Aye, Captain Camplin's taking his pipes round to Peak," Father told us. "We may sail with him and trust that our Robert will give us shelter. He should have heard our news from the carter by now."

"It were thee that wanted to go sailing over t' sea," I told Polly.

"Aye," she answered. "Not like this though."

"There's a bit o' worrying news," Father stroked my hair gently. "Sir Rupert cannot be found. It's said that he headed off to York, for he's another smaller house there. Douthwaite is furious and insists that *he* can't do anything for us. I fear we've little hope of quickly getting the money we're owed. We must all fend for ourselves as best we can. This curse, it does seem to . . ."

Mam couldn't believe it. "Now don't *you* start that," she told him wagging her finger in his face. "How many times have you sworn to me that it's nowt but a fairy tale? Captain Camplin and *The Primrose* are our good luck – are they not? You said so yourself!"

"Aye," Father had to smile at the sudden reversal of Mam's belief. He got up from the fire and hugged her tightly. "You are my good luck," he told her. "You and these fine bairns of ours."

I was happy again to be back on *The Primrose* with Joseph and Tommy, and happy to know that my new washed hair shone and even though my gown was patched, it was patched in bonny colours so that I couldn't remember when I'd felt so clean. Dolly had given me her working clogs and sworn that she was pleased to have a reason to wear her best ones every day.

Lyddy set off to walk back to Sandwick, leaving her son to fulfil his duty by Captain Camplin. The ship's master told both him and Joseph that their willingness and seamanship had been good enough for him to count them as crew, and that meant pay at the end of the voyage.

Hester waved us off from St Anne's Staith and Mam thanked her over and over again. I went very watery eyed myself. The loss of my home had left me **dry**-eyed and empty, while the kindness of the fishing folk, who'd little to spare, touched me deeply, making me want to weep.

I stood on the deck of *The Primrose* with Polly beside me, watching the steep cliff sides of Whitby shrink into the distance in the fading light. Although it wasn't far to Peak, Captain Camplin had to go out into the deeper water to avoid the dangerous rocky shore.

I'd have given anything to be turning north and sailing back to Burning Mountain, but I knew that such a thought was stupid. What would we find there if we did?

Aunt Margaret had always been kind, but she did fuss so and she liked her house-place to be kept very spick and span. Last time we'd visited them I was quite small. We'd stayed for two nights then returned home with Mam declaring that she'd had enough o' fuss, fuss, fuss. What would it be like to stay for weeks, maybe months and would they want us there for such a time, crowding out their home?

At last I turned away with a sigh and saw that Polly was staring up at the tallest mast in the middle of the ship while the crew hauled on ropes and Captain Camplin roared at them from the bridge. She nudged me and pointed "He's swinging about up there like a squirrel."

"Who?" I asked. Trying to see what she meant.

"Your Tommy!"

"Hush! Not my Tommy," I blushed.

"I swear he'd like t'be," she insisted.

I couldn't resist watching him skilfully unfurling the main sail and letting it down, while Captain Camplin yelled instructions to Joseph who rushed about the deck below, pulling the great sail round and making it fast so that it filled with wind and sent *The Primrose* moving steadily south.

17

At Peak

It was dusk when *The Primrose* sailed into the dock at Peak alum works, carried by the evening tide. We stared up at the great dark bulk of Peak House on the south cliff. It was a fine big mansion belonging to Captain Childs, the Alum Master, surrounded by gardens and built on the high rocky headland that stretched out into the North Sea.

"Like a castle," Polly breathed.

"Aye. You were a bairn, Polly, when we last came to visit," Mam reminded us.

"I can remember it," Polly insisted. "Like a castle in a fairytale."

We soon turned our attention away from Peak House, for many of the alum workers came down the steep cliff path to meet us. They'd seen *The Primrose* from afar and curiosity brought them hurrying down. *The Primrose* was soon surrounded by small rowing boats.

Uncle Robert clambered aboard, not at all surprised to see us. "I told our Margaret that you might be here. It'd make sense, I told 'er. We got yer message at noon and I damn near set straight off to Whitby t' see if I could find yer."

"And can yer do with us turning up s' desperate at your door?" Mam's voice had gone very shaky again.

Robert wrapped his arms around her. "O' course we can. Our Margaret's been nagging and nagging me, wishing to see these lasses," he winked at us, and Mam was off sobbing again and wetting his shoulder.

It was a very steep climb up to the workers' cottages and I kept glancing back to see *The Primrose* anchored out in the sea roads with Joseph and Tommy still aboard.

Though Captain Childs was disappointed that our cargo wasn't coal, still he agreed to buy the London urine. Though his works were mainly using kelp, his supplies of seaweed were low and urine would be better than nothing. By the time we reached the rocky ledge with its row of houses and smoking clamps above it was growing dark and we were exhausted.

"Is this cliff safe?" I caught Father by the sleeve, suddenly seeing again our crumbling cottages and toppling clamps.

"Aye honey," he whispered. "Well, it's as safe as any alum worker's haunt."

Then I forgot my fears and felt relieved as Aunt Margaret fussed and fretted over us, kissing us and crying out her thanks for our survival. It was clear that we were very welcome, at least for a while.

"I was stuffing more mattresses," she told us, waving her arms at the sea of straw that filled her house-place. "I thought you would be here tomorrow and I wanted all to be neat and ready for you."

Mam kissed her again. "Just to be safe and warm here with you is like heaven," she murmured. "I can't tell you what heaven it is."

That night we did manage to get to sleep, even though I was squashed together with Polly on one of Aunt Margaret's narrow, hastily stuffed mattresses. When I woke up in the morning, I thought for a moment that I was safe back at home on Burning Mountain. I poked my elbow into Polly's ribs. "Go, fetch the mule!" I murmured.

Then I sat up and looked around me, puzzled. It was clean and cosy in Aunt Margaret's house-place, and she was up and had built up her fire, the kettle swinging over it, hooked on to the reckon. But even though it all looked so warm and bright, my heart sank as the frightening memories of the last two days flooded back into my mind.

"Not Burning Mountain," I whispered. "No Burning Mountain left . . . all gone."

"You fetch t' mule," Polly murmured,

"No," I spoke sharply then. "There *is* no mule, it's dead I'd think. Dead and gone and everything else with it."

Polly suddenly sat up remembering it all. "Patience," she said. "Will she be dead?"

I could do nothing but shrug my shoulders, hearing again the terrible cries that had come from the stable block, and seeing once more the glowing clamps toppling down. "You never liked her," I said.

"No," Polly admitted. "I didn't, but I wouldn't wish her dead."

Mam came into the house-place with a pail of water. "Right now, lasses," she said. "Get up and we'll find some work t' do. It's best thing I swear, it'll take our minds off our troubles and leastways we'll do our best t' pay our way."

"Now tha's no burden," Aunt Margaret insisted. "Let the lasses sleep after what they've been through."

"No," Mam insisted. "Come on, get up lasses. Yer don't want those legs stiffening up!"

We got up willingly enough and ate some of Aunt Margaret's fresh oatcakes. "Now then," Mam asked. "What can they do to be useful? They're fine seaweed pickers and they can do the burning."

"Well," Aunt Margaret looked hesitant. "If they're really willing, there is summat that's needed badly, though I daresay they won't relish it. There's just one lad left that collects the urine from the villages with a cart but he's broken his leg and cannot get about."

I looked at Polly, and Polly looked at me, then suddenly we burst out laughing.

Woman Making Oat Cakes

"Whatever's got into them?" Aunt Margaret was puzzled at the way we howled. "We've been taking turns to do it," she said. "And it's quite a struggle, for we've to leave the other jobs undone, but I wouldn't blame you lasses if you don't fancy . . ."

We both jumped up from the table and kissed Aunt Margaret. "We'll take the cart round and it'll be a pleasure," I told her.

She smiled at Mam surprised.

"We're the famous Collecting Ladies, didn't you know?" Polly giggled.

And strangely enough, though the route and cottages were unfamiliar, just at that moment to be out in the fresh air, trundling along the cliff paths with a cart full of piss, seemed to be the best job in the world.

That evening Joseph and Tommy came up the cliff path to see us. Joseph proudly handed over to Father the payment that Captain Camplin had made to him.

Father hesitated, but we all knew that the few shillings were badly needed. Father's hand at last closed over the coins. "Tha's acting like a man, our Joseph," he said.

Captain Camplin had offered Joseph and Tommy a place amongst his crew for the next voyage. He was determined to sail *The Primrose* up to the River Tyne and come back with a cargo of coal, as all the alum works were now desperately in need of the fuel. There should be good money in it.

"But up to Newcastle," Mam was fretful. "That's where the press-gang's gone," she cried. "Y're determined to get in their way!"

But Joseph was keen to go. "Captain Camplin is clever and cunning Mam," he told her. "We've heard the press-gang've gone up the River Tyne, seeking for the keelboatmen, who bring coal down river from the mines. They've not had much success in ports, so now they try inland."

"But that means even less coal coming out o' Newcastle," Father was puzzled.

"Aye," Tommy grinned wickedly. "So Captain Camplin knows that if he can manage to get a load, it'll fetch the highest possible price."

"Aye well," Father sighed. "We've nowt to offer here. Captain Camplin seems to be turning pirate more than merchantman, but mebbe y're as safe with him as anywhere."

Both lads laughed. "He *is* more of a pirate," said Joseph, "but at least he treats his men decent and pays us fair. We've faith in his seamanship – we'll not be caught."

"You see that yer not," Mam growled.

We went down to the dock the following morning to wave them off. I knew that I'd miss Tommy as much as I'd miss Joseph and I'd worry about them both.

18
The Old Man

All through the winter months we stayed with our aunt and uncle doing our best to help them and work hard, but it was cramped in their little house-place and freezing cold outside. Father was very quiet and we could feel his unhappiness, the only thing that really seemed to rouse him was when Uncle Robert took him into the boiler house and shared his secrets, showing how he was managing to use kelp instead of urine in some of the boiling pans.

Every few weeks Father went off to Whitby to see if there was news of Sir Rupert. Each time he came back unsatisfied, looking greyer and sadder than ever. He brought us news of Annie and her sons who were living with her sister in Whitby, but they were very cramped and short of food. Henry's leg had mended, but crooked. Father sighed. "He'll never run wi' a barrow again," he said.

I felt a great sadness to think of the strong young man so stricken.

"Can he still play his fiddle?" I asked.

"Oh aye," said Father. "He's making a few pennies playing in Whitby Market."

It was horrible to think of him playing while others danced and he could not, but I guessed that being able to make his music was more important to Henry than anything else.

All the old workers from Burning Mountain were suffering hardship and desperate for the money they were owed. "Douthwaite's been offered the manager's job up at Boulby

Works," Father told us. "So the man's doing all right for himself and I can't see him bothering wi' us."

It was early in April that a fast sailing brig arrived at Peak on the evening tide, dropping anchor close to the dock. Father stood on the ledge of the cliff looking down through the fading light.

I went to stand beside him. "Has coal arrived?" I asked him, knowing how eagerly the manager at Peak was looking each day for such a cargo.

He scratched his head, puzzled. "That's no coal brig," he said. "That's no merchantman of any kind that I know of."

I could see a rowing boat heading for the dock, with three men as passengers. We watched as they clambered out and started slowly ascending the cliff path. There was something secretive about the hurry and silence of it all that made me think that we should not be watching.

I grabbed Father's sleeve. "We shouldn't look," I whispered. "Are they bringing in the gin?"

"Nay!" Father shook his head. "They'd hover out in the sea roads till darkness falls for that."

The smaller boat returned to the brig, then came back twice more to shore with three other passengers and a large quantity of baggage. Father and I watched as a coach and four came slowly down the cart track from Peak House, stopping by the steep cliff stairs. The three cloaked men who'd arrived first appeared at the top of the stairs. One of them looked old or ill, leaning heavily on the other two, all muffled in hat and cloak. They got into the carriage and were taken swiftly back to Peak House.

Father shook his head. "Must be the owner's father-in-law," he said. "Margaret told me that he lived in Lincolnshire. Mebbe they've sailed round from Grimsby."

He took my hand and we wandered back to the cottage, a good smell of stewed vegetables drawing us in. "Look's like the father-in-law's arrived by sea," he told Margaret and Mam.

"By sea?" Margaret looked surprised, then suddenly curious. "*The Swallow*? Is it *The Swallow* come back?"

Father shrugged his shoulders, but Uncle Robert got up from the settle, knocking the tobacco out of his pipe in an agitated way. "I'll go and have a look," he told his wife.

He was back in a moment, eyes wide with excitement. "Aye, it's *The Swallow*. I'm sure of it."

"Has the old man come back then?" Margaret asked.

"We did see an old man," I told them. "He was wrapped up in a great cloak, and his back was bent. It was hard for him getting up the steps."

Margaret and her husband both looked at each other, raising their brows and sighing. Mam put down the old bed-gown that she stitched. "What does it mean?" she asked.

"All sit down and eat," Margaret told us. "I think we'd best tell them, Robert. We don't want them saying the wrong thing to anyone."

We gathered round the table then, full of curiosity.

"You know who the Alum Master's daughter married?" Margaret asked.

Father nodded vaguely. "Some gentleman clergyman isn't it?"

"I thought someone told me it was a doctor?" Mam frowned.

"He's both clergyman and doctor," Margaret told us. "And his name is the Reverend John Willis. His father Francis is clergyman and doctor too, though the Reverend Francis is very old now."

"So he's the old man!" I cried, thinking that I'd understood.

"Well, I don't know," Mam sighed. "Why do they bring the old fellow by boat at night and make him walk all the way up that steep path?"

"Ask why indeed?" asked Margaret, looking very mysterious.

There was silence for a moment, then Uncle Robert spoke again. "We always speak o' this visitor as the old man and that's on Captain Childs' strict orders. Y' must be careful to do the same, but Captain Childs can't stop the whispers!"

We were all wide-eyed and listening now. "It's the free-traders!" Polly suggested. "They hide their stuff in Peak House!"

Aunt Margaret snorted with laughter, "Y're partly right lass," she agreed. "The kitchens and pantries up there are full o' fine goods that oughtn't t' be there, but that's kept below stairs. It's what's going on above stairs that's the biggest secret. Doctor John is a mad doctor and he brings his most important patient here for rest and quiet and a bit o' sea air."

"Some say the scent of stale urine does no harm either!" Uncle Robert chuckled.

"Who is it? This patient?" Mam thumped the table, unable to bear the suspense anymore.

"The most important patient that any mad doctor could possibly have," Aunt Margaret suddenly whispered. "Most important in all the realm."

Suddenly Father thought that he understood and his mouth dropped open wide. "No," he breathed. "No surely not!"

"We have not said it," Uncle Robert warned wagging a finger at him.

Mam got up and grabbed hold of Father by his neckerchief. "Who?" she growled.

"Hush Mary . . . it's the king," he whispered. "They've got poor old Farmer George holed up in there. Fancy dragging him up all those steep steps!"

We all gasped and Mam went quite white and sat down with a thump. "Nay," she whispered. "Nay! They'd not do that to him."

"Treatment o' the mad were never gentle," Aunt Margaret shook her head. "And I believe the queen has given permission for these Willis family doctors to do whatever they think is best. The government believe him locked up at Kew with his doctors, that's what the news sheets say, but we mebbe know different."

Polly and I looked at each other, lost for words.

"Now you've not heard it from us," Uncle Robert warned, his voice solemn with the seriousness of it all. "If you ever refer to him, you call him the old man and he's best not referred to at all."

It was hard to sleep that night, thinking that bent and frail figure that we saw rushed up the steps might be his majesty King George. Polly and I tossed and turned and whispered together, even though we were so tired and must get up to start work at dawn.

At last Polly heaved herself up in bed.

"What is it now?" I asked.

"I'm going to get a look at him," she insisted.

"You can't," I told her.

"Yes I can. When we bring the cart back tomorrow we could offer to go seaweed picking, then wander . . . over towards the cliffs beneath the house. Aunt Margaret says he comes to get sea air, and that he's always walking about the gardens. Will you come?"

I couldn't help but smile. "We shouldn't," I said. "But we might try."

19
The King's Shilling

We were up and out of bed the moment that Aunt Margaret started raking the cinders from the fire. We'd finished our collecting by noon and scarce got the patience to eat our bread and cheese before we were offering to go seaweed picking.

"But yer father's gone to Whitby again," Mam sighed, distracted. "He's seeking news o' Sir Rupert. I thought I'd let yer have a bit of time off and go walking up to meet him. You could help him carry some of the goods that he's to buy for Uncle Robert."

I hesitated, unsure what to say, for we'd usually been keen to go walking away from the works to meet Father. These visits to Whitby upset him, for there was never any sign of Sir Rupert and I knew that the errands that he ran for Uncle Robert brought home to him how penniless and dependent we were.

But there was no stopping Polly. "We promised that we'd help old Betty," she lied readily. Betty the seaweed burner had given us a basket of eggs just that morning.

"Aye well, you'd best go in that case," Mam sighed. "For we must do all we can to help. We've nowt to repay folks with but our bent backs."

We went scrambling over the rocks with our baskets on our backs and for a little while we did pick seaweed, fast as we could. But once our baskets were half filled, we headed for the steep slope that lay beneath the terraced, walled gardens of the hall. We marched about beneath them until we were exhausted. There was no sign above us of any old man; the glimpses we got of the gardens looked neat and cared for even in April, but quite deserted. At last we flopped down on the grass, with the high garden wall at our backs, a bit of early spring sunshine warm on our faces.

"It can't be true, anyway," I sighed, frustrated by our fruitless search.

"Nothing goes right for us," Polly complained.

"Nay," I agreed. " 'Tis the curse I'd say. It must be the curse."

"Well then, why does the curse fall on only us and not all alum workers? Why are we more cursed than Aunt Margaret and Uncle Robert?"

I shook my head and sighed.

"I'm sick of doing things Aunt Margaret's way," Polly admitted. "Put your clogs to the side of the hearth! Rake out the cinders! Now collect the ashes! Feed the hens a bit o' grit!"

"Hush!" I told her. I knew that this was ungrateful but I did understand just what she meant. These days at Peak seemed somehow to be getting more difficult than ever, we never could forget that it was their home, and their food that we ate. Mam was snappy and Father got quieter every day.

"I wish we were back at Burning Mountain," I sighed.

"What?" Polly screeched. "You want to live in a pile of mud and stones, with nowt to eat and nowhere to even work."

"Yes," I said. "I think I'd rather."

Polly pushed her hand through my arm and leant her head on my shoulder. "So would I," she murmured.

We both leant back against the wall then and somehow in the warm spring sunshine we nodded off to sleep. I woke later with a jolt to find that the sun had started to sink towards the west. I opened my eyes and couldn't think where I was for a moment, or why I could see a face hanging far above me but upside down.

I gasped and then sat up. As I twisted round to look up at the sturdy walls of the garden above us I realised somebody was looking directly down on us from above. It was indeed the face of an old man, but not moving at all, standing still as a statue.

"Polly, Polly," I whispered, nudging her.

She sighed, yawned and opened her eyes. "I was dreaming that I saw the king," she murmured.

"I think perhaps you did," I hissed.

Suddenly she was wide awake and on her feet. We both stood looking upwards. The face looked steadily back at us. The man was old, with rather bulging eyes and he wore a black hat and cloak; well wrapped up for such a fine spring afternoon.

"Say something," Polly whispered.

My mind went blank. What should we say to somebody that we thought might be the king? "Curtsey," I hissed.

We both picked up our skirts and curtsied, bending deeply down to the ground and then rising up again. Still the face never moved. "Is it a statue?" I murmured.

"Not sure," Polly said. I was beginning to feel that we never should have come, but Polly seemed to get a sudden inspiration.

"We'll sing his song," she said.

"What?"

"You know," she said. Then she pulled herself up very tall, took a deep breath and started singing:

> "God save our gracious King,
> Long live our noble King,
> God save our King."

Still the face didn't move or change, but I could think of nothing else to do, so I joined in.

"Send him victorious
Happy and glorious,
Long to reign over us,
God save our King.

There was a moment of silence when we finished, but then suddenly the face above us was wreathed in smiles, head nodding, hands clapping. We smiled up at him delighted and curtseyed again. When he stopped clapping we shuffled backwards a little way, knowing that you should never turn your back on the king. But as we still watched him, our hearts thumping in our chests, we saw that his hand was outstretched over the top of the wall. Two silver coins came tumbling down from above, landing at our feet. We pounced on them immediately, snatching up one each.

Then a gale of wild laughter came from the old man as we stood there, clutching the coins.

"Now you've taken the king's shilling! What what!" he bellowed, still howling with laughter.

We both dropped our coins as though they were red hot.

"What have we done?" Polly went white. "We've gone and taken the king's shilling. Have we got ourselves impressed?"

"Nay, surely not," I said. "They'd not want lasses in the navy."

"No – no, they wouldn't," Polly agreed, relieved.

When we looked up again the face had vanished and all was silent. We stood there waiting for a while, but never saw the face again.

"Did we dream that?" I muttered.

"The shillings are still here on the ground," said Polly.

"A shilling is a shilling," I said. "And Father could do with two shillings very much."

We picked up our coins. Polly bit hers. "Perhaps these king's shillings are different, they might bring us luck," she said.

As we went back to Aunt Margaret's in the growing dark, I couldn't stop myself trembling a little. "Was it him?" Polly kept asking. "Was it really him?"

"I don't know," was all that I could reply.

But as we drew close the sound of merriment inside made us stop and smile at each other. "Father's back," I said. "Is that him laughing?"

"Aye," said Polly. "That's his laugh all right."

I smiled at that. "I've not heard him laugh since Burning Mountain went down," I said.

"What'll we say about our shillings?" Polly asked. "Will they be angry with us?"

"They might," I agreed. "But Father needs 'em bad, we must give 'em to him. Shall we say Betty paid us?"

Polly had run out of ideas. "She'd never give us that much."

But just at that moment there was another wild burst of laughter from the house-place and it was certainly Father's laugh again. "Has he been drinking?" I asked fearfully, wondering if despair had driven my father to do such a thing.

"Nay, not Father," Polly was shocked. "He'd never spend Uncle Robert's money on ale."

We heard Mam laughing too then and knew that Father couldn't be drunk. Curiosity got the better of us and we just went in.

Father was sitting at the table and he had got a mug of ale in his hand. Uncle Robert was raising his mug to him and Mam and Margaret were both cheerfully raising mugs to their lips.

"What is it?" we asked. Had they all gone mad with the worry of it all?

"Here lasses, come and give us a kiss," Mam cried, banging down her mug and rushing at us both. "We're off back . . . back to Burning Mountain."

"What!"

"How?" We couldn't believe what they were saying.

"Aye, it's true," Mam hugged us. "Sir Rupert's back in Whitby and he's paid a bit o' what he owes us. He's heard how yer father led workers t' safety that terrible night and wishes him to take charge of starting up the alum workings again. Father's acting manager instead o' Douthwaite. What d'yer think o' that?"

We stared open mouthed at this good fortune. It was too much to happen all in one day and we just couldn't speak.

"Why bless 'em," Aunt Margaret cried. "Look at their faces. Now, lasses, have yer lost yer tongues?"

Mam stroked my cheek. "All our troubles are over," she said.

"But . . . when shall we go?" I gasped.

"In t' morning," Mam's face was pink with excitement. "Sir Rupert's paid the carter to take us there."

"But where can we live?" Polly's eyes were suddenly full of doubt and I knew that she saw the tumbling walls of our cottage again.

"New cottages will be built," said Father, "but 'til that be done, we'll live in Whingate Hall."

"What?" I turned to Polly and her mouth dropped open, then suddenly she was gasping and laughing with delight. "Lady Nan, Lady Nanny Goat," she cried, kissing me over and over again.

"Sir Rupert's to have a fine new house built for him, much further back from the cliff edge," said Father. "And don't get too excited lasses, for Whingate Hall'll not be as it was. It's standing right there on the cliff edge now, but they believe it's secure for a while."

But Polly and I would not listen to his cautions, we were wild with excitement and grabbed each other and danced about Aunt Margaret's house-place. "I said these shillings would be lucky shillings," Polly howled.

"What shillings is this?" Mam asked.

We stopped our jigging then and handed over our coins to Father. It didn't seem to matter now, whether we'd be in trouble or not.

"We sang for the old man and he threw us a shilling each," I told them. Such a thing must be unimportant compared to the news that we were to go back to our home.

"He said we'd taken the king's shilling," Polly added. "And he laughed at us."

Suddenly Uncle Robert started laughing. "They took the king's shilling," he roared pointing at us. "They took the king's shilling!" Everybody else joined in, screaming with laughter until you'd have thought we were all going mad.

20

Return to Burning Mountain

We couldn't sleep much that night and we were all awake and bustling about in candlelight before the sun rose.

"Well, at least we've no packing to fret about," Mam joked. "That's one good thing to be said for having nowt but the clothes y' stand up in."

"Now that's not quite true," Aunt Margaret insisted. "There's a basket of eggs that I've set aside and two laying hens packed into a crate. Robert insists that you take the young nanny; she's due to give birth soon, so that will start you off afresh and there'll soon be milk. Why . . . what is it?"

Tears had sprung to all our eyes and Mam lurched towards her sister-on-law, hugging her fiercely. "What ever would we'er done wi'out you?"

As soon as I could get to her I went to hug my aunt as well. I couldn't find the right words to say, but clung to her tightly in silence, remembering how bitterly we'd complained about her yesterday.

"Now that's enough o' that," she spoke with warm common sense. "There's too much to do for us to be larking about like this. I daresay y'd do the same for us, should we be shuffled into the sea, and mebbe that day will come."

"Lady Hilda save you from it!" Mam spoke with vehemence.

The carrier's cart arrived soon after sun-up and we were bundled inside with the goat and hens and bumping on our way over the cliff tops towards Whitby Town. We stopped in

Whitby to buy picks and shovels and to meet up with Annie and her sons. Hester had heard the news that we were returning home and she came running down Kirkgate to the Inn Yard to greet us, her arms piled high with clothing. There were new aprons for us and Mam, and a strong pair of fustian breeches for Father. Rachel, Hester, and her daughters had been stitching all through the winter months for us.

There were hugs and greetings again when Annie turned up with her sons, to join us. I hated the painful way Henry dragged his leg. With many waves and cries of gratitude to the fisher wives we rumbled away from Whitby and on towards Burning Mountain, Annie and her sons following behind us in another cart. There were no complaints when we all got out to walk up Lythe Bank. As we scrambled back into the cart for the last bit of the journey, my stomach pulled itself tight with longing, for the sight of Burning Mountain.

From the distance the first glimpse of our home was puzzling. "What place is this?" I asked.

Mam shook her head and Father stared ahead in silence.

"This is Burning Mountain," Jack Carter told us.

"But where . . .?" Polly stammered.

"Look," said Mam, pointing ahead uncertainly. "Is that Whingate Hall?"

We stared in disbelief. It was Whingate Hall, we could tell that by the shape of the house and the six chimneys, but this Whingate Hall stood so very close to the cliff edge that no sign of wall or garden remained.

"I forgot," I whispered, feeling frightened by the strangeness of it all. "I forgot where the gardens had gone."

"Aye," Mam shrugged her shoulders. "Over the edge," she said.

Father shook his head. "I knew t'would be bad," he whispered, "But . . . I didn't think . . ."

"Never mind," Mam came in with determination. "We are

back and this is our home and we shall damned well make a good fist of it. I'm not turning back!"

As we drew closer we began to realise that Whingate Hall was not at all the place that it once had been. It had gone through the worst weather without fires or cleaning or care of any kind and much of it was ruined. We got down from the cart and stumbled forwards stiff-legged. Though the stone façade was still very fine looking, the windows were broken and thick clumps of grass had seeded themselves on the great flight of steps. Through force of habit we wandered around the side of the house looking for the back door. I remembered from before the warmth of the kitchen with its great fireplace and bread ovens and game-birds turning on the spit.

We stood back as Father came forwards with the keys that Sir Rupert had given him. He glanced at Mam, unsure what to do. "Should we go in the front?"

"No," Mam told him. "The back's further away from the cliff, that's got t' be better, and maybe we'll feel more comfortable in t' servants rooms."

So after a few false tries Father managed to turn the key in the rusted lock, and we all crowded in after him. Of course there was no fire, or gleaming brass gate, we knew not to expect that, but the sight of desolation inside the place was still shocking.

"I should've known," Father whispered, trying to calm himself. "Should've expected it."

Sir Rupert had sent his servants to strip the place. Every scrap of decent furniture had gone; all that was left was a broken upturned table in the corner of the kitchen and two chairs with broken legs. Everything was covered in thick grey mud and dust. It was freezing cold and damp. Most of the windows were broken and a fine sea breeze was whooshing through.

We followed Father in silence, nobody spoke and we

wandered from room to room, remembering the glimpses that we'd had in the past of this once fine house. Every room was filthy and destroyed; the great expanses of the ballroom and the entrance hall seemed worse for the very hugeness of the wreckage that was there.

"Tha wouldn't want to dance here now, Lady Nan," Polly murmured.

Without a word we all turned and wandered back to the kitchen. Father sat down on the back doorstep, careless of all the mess. He stared ahead in blank despair, still saying nothing. Mam went to sit beside him taking tight hold of his hand.

"I was flattered," he murmured. "I was so damned pleased and flattered when Sir Rupert wished me manager. What a fool I was! I didn't think what I'd be manager of. A sea o' rubble and ruin."

Mam just held him tightly, her determination seemed to have seeped away again and she could find nothing to say.

We left them there.

"I want to look at Alum Row," I whispered, trying hard to stop my chin from trembling. I took Polly's arm and we wandered away around the side of the house, going as far as we dared so that we could look down upon the wreckage and mud that had once been our real home.

The mess beneath us was dreadful, crumbled walls, and smashed chimneys were deep in shale and mud. All the carefully built brick alum culverts and wooden channels were cracked and useless. We stared miserably down at it all.

"It was better at Aunt Margaret's," Polly sighed.

"Aye," I whispered. "That's truth!"

Then as we stood there the sun came out from behind a patch of cloud and a lark started to sing, rising up from the heather warbling cheerfully. Despite the destruction, my spirits rose a little and I looked again and saw it differently.

The sea was still the deepest dark blue and the grass fresh and green, the whin-flowers just coming into bloom, made golden patches in amongst the mess.

"This *is* still our home," I said.

"Aye it is," Polly agreed.

We'd looked out on to those gorgeous spring colours every year since we could remember.

Polly sighed. "The whins are still here for us and look – look down there! Can you see what I can see?" she cried, grabbing my arm excitedly. "There's food here after all."

I looked where she was pointing and the small bud of happiness that I'd felt seemed to grow inside me. Close to the rubble-dump of our old cottages we could see a clearly marked off square of fresh green growth.

"Our cabbages!" I cried. "Cabbages and kale."

It was strange that such a small thing should make us feel so much better, but it did. The powerful landslip had destroyed our homes and the works from top to bottom, but still Father's careful autumn plantings were pushing their way up through the shaley soil.

Then another movement far below caught our eye. Someone was picking a way through the mud, slowly climbing up the steep messy cliff-side towards us. As we watched them come closer, we saw that it wasn't just one person, but several. They were fisherwomen, we could tell from their frilled bonnets; they came striding up the slope, their arms laden with baskets and bags. Then the woman who led them looked up at us and started waving.

"Lyddy . . . it's Lyddy!" I cried.

We turned and ran straight back to the house. Father hadn't moved, though Mam and Annie had carried a mud-caked wooden bucket to the pump. "There's water at least," she was saying.

"Mam, Mam," we cried. "Lyddy Welford's marching up

the cliff side with a besom over her shoulder and a bucket in her hand. There's half o' Sandwich Bay coming with her."

Mam stopped her pumping and Father looked up at us puzzled. He rose to his feet and at once they all followed us round the side of the house.

The women were much closer now and we could see that they carried cooking pots, loaves of bread, warm patched quilts and goodness knows what else. Behind them marched a train of fishermen, carrying shovels and spades.

"Bless 'em!" Mam murmured. "Bless 'em!"

21

In Action Again

There was little time for greetings, for Lyddy and her friends walked straight into Whingate kitchen and set about fixing the mess right away. Father was bewildered and Mam full of gratitude.

"Bless y' Lyddy, but you can't spare time to work up here, you've got your bait to gather and lines to fix."

"That can be set aside for just one day," Lyddy told us. "We heard Sir Rupert'd sent for you, though how he thinks you'll manage here I don't know. There'll be no fishing done tonight; our fellows've come up here to help thee get started. Now then Thomas, they'll do whatever they can to start the workings off again."

Father looked amazed. "We can't let you do it," he said shaking his head in disbelief.

Francis Welford was a tall, broad fisherman who you wouldn't want to argue with. He pointed to Polly and me. "If it were not for these lasses o' yourn, and the warning that they brought us, half o' Sandwick Bay would be far away on a man o' war by now. We don't forget a thing like that."

Father turned to us and suddenly his eyes were full of tears. "That were the best day's work you ever did, my lasses," he said. "I'm so proud of you."

I'd never seen him look at us quite like that before.

"Take these fish-faces away with yer," Lyddy laughed. "Leave us women to sort out here. This'll not last long, Thomas, so make the most of it. Take these fellows away and put them to work!"

"You're going to work with us?" Henry Knaggs looked stunned.

"You can't shovel lad, not with that leg," Annie interrupted.

"No," Father spoke with his usual determination again. "But he can tell these lads what to do all right!"

"Come on then, Alum Master," Francis Welford would not be put off. "Tell us where to start, man!"

"A clamp," said Father faintly. "We should find brushwood for kindling and build a clamp. I think there'll be enough loose alum shale to start us off."

"Have we plenty o' shovels?" asked Francis.

"Aye," Father acknowledged.

"Then let us get going, man, for we've no time to waste."

Mam sent us girls out to scavenge coal and wood, while Lyddy and her friends started on the kitchen. If fisherwives set about doing something, they do it good and proper and they do it fast. When we returned, dragging half-filled sacks of coal and kindling, things looked very different. Whingate kitchen walls were scrubbed, the stone paved floor was scoured and the fireplace and ovens had been raked out and scraped clean.

"Now that's just what we need, lasses," Lyddy grabbed our bags and soon had a fire going that warmed the oven and the bake-stone. A good fish stew was soon bubbling away on the reckon and the smell of it made me realise how exhausted and hungry I was.

"How am I going to get the hang of using these fancy ovens?" Mam wondered.

"Oh, I can show you well enough," Lyddy insisted. "Did I never tell how I was scullery-maid here, when I was nobbut a lass?"

"You worked here? Never!" Mam gasped.

"Not for long," Lyddy laughed. "Bait-gathering suited me

a deal better than scouring pans, I found that out soon enough, but I've not forgotten how to rake this thing out and set the fire."

They left us in the evening with full bellies and mattresses to sleep on. We all slept together in the warm kitchen, and bare though it was, it was blissful to have such space after the crowding at Aunt Margaret's.

"Fresh stuffed mattresses and fresh hope too," said Father cheerfully. His eyes were drooping with weariness, but there was a new energetic glint there. "Aye," said Mam. "It's going t' be hard work and no mistake, but we can do it. I know we can. You get those workings going and me and Annie'll make a home for us in this crumbled shell."

"Can we make the ballroom fine?" I asked, memories of Sir Rupert's daughters still refusing to go away.

Both Mam and Father laughed at me, sighing and shaking their heads.

"I wouldn't mind tripping up and down in that ballroom, lass," Annie told me. "I'd need a fine strapping lad to partner me though."

We laughed again at the thought of Annie doing that.

The following weeks were hard and bitter work, but at least we didn't have to go off collecting urine, for that would only be needed for the finishing work, and it would be a long time before there'd be lead pans of alum liquor boiling again. Father and the men were busy digging steeping-pits, while some of the lads fuelled the one clamp that we'd got going, and set to work on another one. Father made Henry his assistant and, despite his troublesome leg, he seemed to be everywhere that he was needed, giving out information and advice.

"I used to hate those stinking clamps," Polly said, standing hands on hips staring up at them. "Now I love to see the smoke curling up puthering all around. We're really Burning Mountain again."

I knew just what she meant.

Some of the old alum workers who'd not found proper work since the landslip heard of our return and started coming back to join us. They arrived crammed into carts, skinny and desperate, some arriving with nowt but the clothes on their backs that they'd worn on that dreadful day. We made them as welcome as we could and helped them to clean out and repair the old sitting-rooms and living-rooms. Whingate Hall was slowly inhabited again, growing like a bees' nest, with busy workers buzzing in and out. We'd done well to claim the kitchen and Mam set about baking bread and oatcakes for all, exchanging the food for work and favours. She even scrubbed and mended some of the broken utensils that had been left in the old dairy, ready to start making goat's cheese. Annie brewed ale in the sitting-room, scoured buckets and flagons all standing about and a fine strong smell of fermenting barley arose. We soon started to call it Annie's Alehouse.

Sir Rupert sent stone breakers to hack up big chunks of stone and spread it to make us a decent new road. Carpenters and bricklayers arrived by the cartload, with timber and bricks, all paid for by Sir Rupert. They set to work on a new boiler house and smithy, for the work sheds must be built before anything else. Barrowmen and pickmen came daily, walking over from Lythe.

Every afternoon Mam sent us down the cliff-side scavenging. At first we didn't want to do it, but soon began to find that there was joy in the small bits and pieces that we collected. We gathered coal and wood, and harvested the cabbages and kale from Father's half-buried plot. We managed to capture a few scraggy chickens that had somehow survived the winter. We dug out dirty alum crystals from shallow pits, that could be washed and sold locally. We sent a

Stone-breakers on the Road

good parcel to Hester and Rachel as we'd promised. Sometimes we walked to Sandwick Bay and returned with parcels of fish heads and tails, to make a good strengthening broth.

One afternoon we were digging away when we heard the wickering snort of a horse.

"What's that?" I stared about us, but couldn't see any riders.

"I know that bray," Polly said. "That's no horse."

She stood up and clicked her fingers. "Come on, mokey, come on, mokey!" she cried and to our great delight an answering wicker came again and Patience emerged, looking very puzzled, from behind a large whin-bush.

"Oh no," we groaned. "Not her again. How ever are we going to catch her?"

But Patience came straight to us, standing obediently still, nuzzling at our hands, as she'd never done before. I took off my apron and tied the strings around her neck like a halter, while she stood there letting us stroke her sides. Her coat was matted and grazed, thick with mud; her ribs stood out above her shrunken belly.

"She's glad to be caught," Polly stroked her neck.

Another treasure that we found was Mam's old spinning wheel. It was buried deep in spent alum shale, and it took us two weeks to get it out, working for a good while each day, digging and scraping carefully round it. We didn't say anything to Mam, then one day we appeared in Whingate Hall yard with it, and you should have seen her face, she didn't know whether to laugh or cry. Spokes were smashed and the wood was dented, but father mended it up and we soon had it polished and in working order.

"Now then," said Mam smiling and delighted. "All we need is a fleece and I shall be in action again."

22

A Birthday Surprise

The weeks flew by so hard we worked, and soon my birthday drew near once again.

"I can't believe it," I said to Polly as we sat in the sun on the kitchen doorstep. "It were only a year ago that I sat up there picking berries, looking down on Whingate Hall, wishing that I lived here. Now I do and I wish I were safe back in Alum Row."

"Aye," Polly replied with feeling. "And I wished to go away over the sea, and I've had enough o' that too."

"I doubt Mam will give us the afternoon off this year," I sighed.

"No," Polly agreed thoughtfully. "But . . . maybe . . ."

"Maybe what?" I asked.

"Never you mind," Polly told me firmly, scrambling to her feet and going inside. "You stay here and mind yer own business if you want a birthday treat!"

I started to get up to follow her, but then smiled and sat down again. Maybe she was going to try to persuade Mam to let us have the day off after all. I shouldn't interfere with that.

My birthday dawned and nothing was said about a holiday, so I sighed a little to myself as I carried on my usual work, scavenging coals down on the cliff-side. Polly sat beside me staring out to sea while I grubbed about in the shale.

"You're not picking up much," I told her sharply. "Father says they're needing more coal every day now, and they'll not be able to set up the new boiling pans without it."

"Huh!" Polly grinned, then suddenly she was scrambling to her feet. "I'm on the look-out for coal," she said. "I've got a much better way to get it, and I think **I'm** succeeding. Look up and see for theesen!"

I turned around thinking that she was teasing me, but then I saw sails, far out to sea, heading towards Burning Mountain.

"Can it be . . .?" I gasped.

"Aye," Polly grinned. "*The Primrose*."

"But how . . .?"

"This is yer birthday treat," Polly laughed. "I've been keeping it secret . . . we all have. Captain Camplin managed to get a good cargo o' coal and they took it to Peak, but Uncle Robert's insisted that they bring on just a bit here to help us get the pans going. The carter brought us news and we kept it to ourssens so you'd have a fine birthday surprise. Joseph and Tommy are coming to celebrate. Look, they're all expecting *The Primrose*!"

I turned back amazed towards Whingate Hall and saw that Father was leading Patience down the hill, followed by the other six mules that Sir Rupert had sent to occupy the new stables. Mam and Annie and many of the other workers followed, clambering down the slope. I left my bag of scavenged coals and set off too, trying to follow where the old pathway had once been. Polly skidded along behind me, and soon we ran out on to the scar. I stared about us then in dismay. "How can they get here?" I asked. The landslip had covered the channel that once cut through the rocky scars.

"Father says they'll manage," Polly would do nothing but smile.

They did manage, but with difficulty. *The Primrose* had to anchor out in deep water, bringing loads of coal to the beach in their two small rowing boats. Then the mules were loaded up to carry it back and forth up the hill. Everyone helped and by dusk we'd managed the last load and a decent stack of coal stood beside the new and growing walls of the boiler house.

Both Joseph and Tommy kissed me and wished me happy birthday. They were full of the frightening adventures they'd had with Captain Camplin, just missing the press-gang at every turn. Joseph had a split ear where a rope had caught him unawares and Tommy had a bullet graze in his leg, from a press-ganger's gun.

"You'll not be going again then?" Mam asked hopefully.

"We will," they both spoke at once and showed the handful of shillings that Captain Camplin had paid them with.

Back at Whingate, a delicious smell of baking drifted from Mam's ovens. Annie came out of the ballroom and closed the damaged door quickly behind her. "Not yet!" she snapped.

"Not yet?" I puzzled.

"Come with me," Polly snatched my hand and pulled me into the sitting room. "We've to dress for dinner."

"What?"

"Take that apron off," she ordered.

I obeyed and saw that she'd made a lovely wreath of wild flowers for me, with bluebells and campions all twined together with ivy, and Mam had stitched a fine new linen pinafore for me, dyed golden by the gorse flowers. I rushed to put them on.

"Now you're a real Lady Nan," Polly laughed.

I kissed her. "I can't believe what a grand day I'm having," I said, and my eyes were full of tears that came from happiness.

"It's not finished yet," she told me, leading the way to the ballroom. "Are you ready now?" she shouted.

"Aye! Aye!" many voices called.

Polly flung open the ballroom doors and such a sight met my eyes. The room was swept and clean, with a fire crackling in the broken hearth. The walls were decorated with sweet scented gorse flowers, gleaming golden in the light of many flickering candles. The broken shutters and cracked glass had been removed and the warm summer's night drifted inside.

Everyone clapped and cheered for me, and Tommy came forward bowing and holding out his hand. "Will m' lady dance?" he begged.

I nodded. I couldn't speak. Henry Knaggs struck up a tune on his fiddle and I forgot my mud-caked feet and my patched and mended skirt and danced joyfully round Whingate ballroom with him.

"Now's my chance," cried Annie. She snatched hold of Joseph who looked startled for just a moment but then bowed and offered her his hand, as everyone else joined in.

I sat up on the cliff top with Polly and Father beside me, watching a small black dot disappearing into the distance. *The Primrose* was going on her way once more, taking our Joseph and Tommy with her.

I sighed for I'd miss them both so much, but my birthday celebrations had left a great warm glow inside me, that I knew would be there for a long, long time.

"Aye, lasses," said Father, his voice deep with satisfaction. "Listen to the busy sounds of picks and shovels, then look down there. I never thought we'd see that sight again – burning clamps, dark red steeping-pits, and a fine new boiler house almost ready to be used."

"It's grand," I told him. "And you've done it all."

"I couldn't have done it without you two," he said and leant over kissing first me, then Polly. I sighed again with joy, but – as we sat there in the sun a bad thought came into my mind that made me sigh yet again and it wasn't with joy this time.

"Father?" I asked. "When y' get yer new boiling pans going, will me an' Polly have t' be the Collecting Ladies again?"

Father smiled, and then he started laughing loudly so that we looked startled at him.

"What?" I cried. "What's funny?"

"Bless you, Nan," he said calming down at last. "What would you say if I said you'd never have to collect stale urine again?"

"What? Never in my life?"

"Never ever again," he said firmly.

"Well, I'd say it were a better birthday present than any I could possibly have."

"Well, it's true," he said and my spirits soared. "Robert's made clear to me the best ways o' using kelp instead o' urine, but there's still trouble finding enough o' the stuff. We've nowhere near enough down on these scars, even if the pickers worked day and night at it!"

I frowned, but Father was still smiling. "Don't fret," he said. "I've been talking to Camplin and he says he's seen boatloads of it coming from far up north in the Shetland Isles."

"So can *we* get it from there?"

"Aye. Camplin's agreed t' fetch one load o' coal, then his next trip will be a load of kelp. He swears they're swimming in the stuff up there and will sell it cheap, glad to get it taken away. Now then, does that make my lasses happy?"

"It does," Polly told him. "I'd say, 'God bless them up in the Shetland Isles!'"

"Aye," I added, "And God bless Captain Camplin too!"

Author's Note

I would like to thank David Pybus for help and advice and kindly sharing his knowledge of the history of alum working and the Whitby area; also Thomas W. V. Roe for information about the Grape Lane riots.

Burning Mountain and its Alum Works are imaginary as are the main characters in the story; however many such works were situated along the North East Coast between Ravenscar and Saltburn.

Peak Works really existed and the remains of the workings can still be seen on the cliff-side, beneath Peak Hall – now the Raven Hall Hotel, Ravenscar. That George III spent time there recovering from his illnesses is local mythology. There seems to be no proof that it really happened, but the daughter of Captain William Childs, owner of the Hall and the alum works, was indeed married to one of the Willis family of doctors to whom the care of George III was given.

Some other incidents in the story reflect real events that took place, though not all in the same year.

In 1830 the workers' settlement and the Alum Works at Kettleness were swept into the sea by a cliff fall. The workers were rescued by an Alum Boat and taken to Whitby,

John Tindale's *Owlers, Hoverer's and Revenue Men*, describes a serious riot that took place in Whitby in 1784 when a mob attacked the press-gang's headquarters and proceeded to pull it down. One man, William Atkinson, was charged with aiding and abetting and was hanged at York in 1790.

Alum Making

The alum shale lies in the "Upper Blue Lias", beneath a layer of earth and ironstone, known as "dogger head". The miners had to remove this layer to get at the grey alum slate. This was dug out, creating a semi-circular shaped quarry, then taken in barrows to a flat ledge where it was piled up into a heap on top of burning brushwood, to form the clamps. These clamps were coated with clay and burned steadily for at least three months, giving off sulphurous fumes. The burnt slate turned to a reddish-yellow and was reduced to about half of its original size.

This roasted shale was then barrowed to steeping pits, dug close-by on the sloping cliff-side, for ease of transport. Water was pumped in and left for three days, then the water carrying the dissolved chemical known as liquor was drawn off and carried down the cliff-side in wooden gutters to the boiler house. Here, with previously reduced liquor called "mothers' being", it was boiled in lead pans to concentrate the solution for about twenty-four hours.

Urine or kelp lees were then added, as a source of ammonia, making crystals form. The crystals were often dissolved again and at this point the success of the work depended very much on the judgement and experience of the workers. When the required density was reached, the liquor was run off from the pans into "roaching casks", great wooden butts constructed so as to be easily taken apart. The liquor was left to cool and crystallize for eight to ten days. At the right time the hoops and staves were removed, and white alum crystals found inside. This is a very basic and simple description of what was a complicated and fascinating process. The workers at the time did not understand the chemical process and had to work by experience, trial and error.

Theresa Tomlinson, 2001
www.theresatomlinson.com

Note on Illustrations

The illustrations are from George Walker's picture book, *Costume of Yorkshire*, first published in 1814. I would like to thank John Capes of Staithes for help in acquiring an 1885 edition of Walker's book, from which the pictures have been reproduced. (email: capes@staithes.fsbusiness.co.uk)

George Walker travelled around Yorkshire during the early years of the 1800's, drawing the working people of the area. I believe these pictures to be as near a true representation of the sort of people I'm writing about, as we can now have. They also include what, to my knowledge, is the only contemporary drawing of alum workings.

Bibliography

The Alum Farm, Robert Bell Turton, printed and published by Horne and Son, Ltd Whitby, 1938

Chapter 4 "Alum and the Yorkshire Coast" by David Pybus and John Rushton, from *The Yorkshire Coast*, ed. David Lewis, published by Normandy Press, 1991

Alum – North East Yorkshire's fascinating story of the first chemical industry, Alan Morrison, published by the author, 7 Broadfern Road, Knowle, Solihull, West Midlands, 1981

"The Uses of Urine" by Jennifer Stead, from *Old West Riding* Vol. 1, No.2, 1981

"The Impress Service in North-East England during the Napoleonic War" by Norman McCord, and "The Noble Ann Affair, 1779" by Tony Barrow, from *Pressgangs and Privateers*, published by Bewick Press, Whitely Bay, 1993

Owlers, Hoverers and Revue Men, by John Tindale, published by Whitby Publishers, 1986